中英雙語典藏版

全球發行量破千萬的不朽之作
被譽為「小聖經」的生命頌詩

先知

The Prophet

黎巴嫩藝術天才與文壇驕子

卡里·紀伯倫

（Kahlil Gibran）——著

曾惠昭——譯　楊宛靜——繪

晨星出版

導讀

《先知》的真理饗宴
文字工作者／李曉菁

　　「你的船已抵達，你必須走了。」女預言家艾蜜特拉說。奧菲里斯城的群眾放下工作，扶老攜幼前來，不捨阿穆斯塔法（Almustafa）離去，唯有艾蜜特拉明瞭，這位上天揀選與鍾愛的先知，為了尋求超越之境，目光不斷望向遠方，搜尋他的船，已經很久了！

　　對土地的熱愛、對群眾的不捨，與前往異地追尋更高境界的想望，多股潮流在阿穆斯塔法心頭激盪。智慧的艾蜜特拉為群眾發言：「我們的愛不會束縛你，我們的需要也不耽擱你」；然而，她為群眾渴求，在阿穆斯塔法離開之前：「對我們說話，給我們真理。」讓這些關於生命的真知灼見，隨著子孫綿延，世代傳遞，永不湮滅。

　　「靈魂綻放自己，像一朵有無數花瓣的蓮花。」猶如蓮花綻放，先知緩緩吐露充滿哲思與詩意的語言，用單純的真理，深入人心。

　　敞開封閉的心，閱讀《先知》，迸發出的，是初戀的美麗悸動。先知要人追隨愛的召喚，當愛神發現你夠資格，自然會前來指引方向，讓你在愛中領略痛苦、釋放慾望，最後成全自己。而當生命出現真愛，先知要兩人彼此相愛，卻不綑綁彼此，就像橡樹與杉樹，同向上爭取陽光，不能在彼此的陰影下成長。

　　先知的語言洋溢溫柔，世界充滿無限包容。快樂與悲傷、理性與熱情、善與惡，這些世俗以為對立的價值觀，在先知眼中，並不相對，也不絕對，關鍵存乎一心。

因此他要人在快樂時省察自己的內心，然後會發現，那曾令你悲傷的，正賦予你快樂；而悲傷的人們，不也正為曾經快樂的事物哭泣。快樂與悲傷，在人心中分享著不可分割的命運，猶如善惡、好壞、正直與不義，用樹根纏繞地心的姿態，相互糾結，互為因果。而當理性與熱情、價值判斷與感官慾望在靈魂的戰場交戰，又該讓哪個支配哪個？

　　徬徨的人們渴望先知的指引，而他卻只是謙卑地提醒：「除了那此刻仍浮動在你們靈魂中的，我還能說些什麼？」那樣的回答，喚起沈默已久的心靈。

　　人們懷抱疑惑前來提問。懷抱乳兒的婦女問孩子、富人問給予、客棧老闆問飲食、農人問工作、泥水匠問房屋、織工問衣服、商人問買賣、法官問罪與罰、律師問律法、演說家問自由、教師問教育、學者問說話、天文學家問時間、青年問友誼、老人問善惡、詩人問美、隱士問歡樂、女祭司問祈禱、老祭司問宗教，二十八篇中，各階層的男女老少，從自己的觀點、職業出發，問的都是環繞自我的話題，然而，他們的疑惑，也是普世人們的疑惑，先知明白，他回答的對象將是全人類，不是一個人。

　　傾聽的人們，在先知的話語中，重估一切的價值與生活方式，傲然直立的人失重跌倒、跌落的人重新攀爬起來，然而，那不是先知的意圖，他掀起的，是一場不偏坦任何一方的心靈交戰，要人們在清晰的真光中審察一切，跌倒與直立的，本是同一個人，而眾人最後要面對的，都是同一個問題，死亡。

　　尼采筆下的覺者查拉圖斯特拉（Zarathustra），因為對人類的愛，背起重荷，深入人群，教導凡人自我超越，必要經歷三個精神發展階段：從負重服從的駱駝期，進入自尊自重的獅子期，最後反璞歸真，進入充滿遊戲熱情與創造力的孩童期，尼采帶來的，是人文主義的復興；紀伯倫筆下的阿穆斯塔法，不隸屬任何教派，懷抱真摯的人道主義，出於愛與不捨，用充滿象徵與譬喻的語言，領人們從出生到死亡，真實面對一項又一項真理，在辯證的過程中，他正視充滿矛盾的現實世界，也對生存在這世界的人們，釋放無盡的寬恕。

讀者很難想像，《先知》中睿智又熱情澎湃的語彙，在紀伯倫十五歲時，已經用阿拉伯文打下底稿。一八八三年一月六日，卡里・紀伯倫（Kahlil Gibran）出生在黎巴嫩山區，一座名為布雪里的平原上。幼年的紀伯倫，在黎巴嫩群山的包圍下度過；青年時期則生活在美國波士頓、紐約，這樣的成長背景，引起傳記家極大的興趣，認為是造成紀伯倫雙重性格的關鍵。生長在宗教氛圍濃厚的家庭，紀伯倫個性中，蘊涵追求自由獨立的因子，一生不斷以文字宣傳革命、宣揚和平之美。矛盾的是，有人讚美其信仰虔敬，也有人貶其為反叛者與異教徒。一九〇一年，他畢業於貝魯特教會大學 Madrasat Al-Hikmat，開始大量以阿拉伯文創作，其中著名的《反叛的精神》，被貼上「危險、叛逆、毒害青年」的標籤，焚於貝魯特市場，紀伯倫也因此被教會除名，開始流亡生涯。

身體的放逐，卻讓他的藝術心靈在歐洲大陸得到激盪。一九〇八年，他移居巴黎，以畫畫維生，曾為羅丹、德布西等人畫像，成為社交界知名人物。兩年後，他移居紐約，直到一九三一年病逝。在這之間，他發行第一本英文著作《瘋子》（The Madman）；一九二三年，以英文直接創作、五年內經歷五次改寫的《先知》（The Prophet），終於出版，成為紀伯倫的代表作。然而，他的阿拉伯文學創作，早在阿拉伯世界形成一股強大的閱讀風潮，《破折的翅膀》列入中東經典文學；紀伯倫獨特的阿拉伯文體，更被稱為「紀伯倫體」。

在短暫而富影響力的一生，紀伯倫的愛情世界，是人們急於探索的話題。紀伯倫不排斥情愛，承認女性對他的影響，甚至在《先知》第二、三篇，碰觸的就是愛情、婚姻等問題，「當愛召喚你時，追隨它」的告誡猶在耳邊，然而「彼此相愛，但不要使愛成為枷鎖」的回應，或許更能貼近他終身不婚的緣由。他用工作去愛生命，認為透過勞動過程，才能親近生命的內在奧秘，因而，他對婚姻的排拒有了充足的理由，他說，當他投入工作時，可能會好幾天一語不發，沒有女人能夠忍受這樣的另一半。對他來說，「工作是愛的具體化」，而精神與肉體，透過工作，得到聯繫，那是《先知》為什麼說：

生命的確是黑暗，除非有盼望，

所有盼望都是盲目，除非有知識，

所有知識都是枉然，除非有工作，

所有工作都是空虛，除非愛在其中，

當你懷抱愛心工作，才能將你與自己，與人人，與神聯繫在一起。

薄暮已至，告別時刻終於到來，奧菲里斯城的民眾，不到與阿穆斯塔法的別離，不明白愛的深度。群眾從盲目耳聾，到聽見、看見、感受到彼此生命攸關，已然費去許多個日出日落、春夏秋冬、生離死別。阿穆斯塔法離去，可是應許猶在：「別忘了，我必再度歸來……另一個女人將生下我」，終成為《先知》閱讀者，低迴不已的詠歎。

目録

01
船來了

阿穆斯塔法集所有榮寵於一身，他是當代的曙光，在奧菲里斯城待了十二個寒暑，等船來接他返回出生之島。

在第十二個年頭，收割月的第七日，他登上城牆外的山頭，遠眺大海，看見他的船隨著薄霧駛來。

他的心門豁地開敞，喜悅奔騰直達海上。他閉起雙眼，在沉靜的靈魂中默禱。

Almustafa, the chosen and the beloved, who was a dawn unto his own day, had waited twelve years in the city of Orphalese for his ship that was to return and bear him back to the isle of his birth.

And in the twelfth year, on the seventh day of Ielool, the month of reaping, he climbed the hill without the city walls and looked seaward; and he beheld the ship coming with the mist.

Then the gates of his heart were flung open, and his joy flew far over the sea. And he closed his eyes and prayed in the silences of his soul.

然而，在他走下山頭時，愁思忽地湧現：

我如何能平靜地離去，不帶走一絲哀愁？不，我無法不帶著精神上的創傷離開這座城。

在此城中，我經歷了痛苦串起的白晝和孤寂綴成的夜晚；試問，誰能了無牽繫地擺脫痛苦和孤寂？

街道上鋪陳著我的思念，山林間穿梭著孩童們赤足行進的身影，我無法全無傷懷地從這些事物中悄然隱退。

今天，我褪下的不是一件外衣，而是親手剝離的一層皮。

置諸身後的也並非一個念頭而已，而是一顆用飢渴凝聚起來的甘甜之心。

然而，我不能再遲疑了。

召喚萬物的大海正召喚著我，我必須啟程了。

因為，我留下來只會僵固凝結，局限在模型之中，儘管時間在夜裏熊熊燃燒。

倘若能將這一切帶走，我會多麼高興，然而，我怎能夠？

唇舌給予聲音飛翔的羽翼，聲音卻無法攜唇舌同行，它必須獨自翱翔天際。

鷹鳥必得離開窩巢，獨自振翅，以期橫越旭日。

現在，他已行至山下，再次轉身望向大海，看見他的船泊進港口，船首站著來自故鄉的水手。

But he descended the hill, a sadness came upon him, and he thought in his heart: How shall I go in peace and without sorrow? Nay, not without a wound in the spirit shall I leave this city.

Long were the days of pain I have spent within its walls, and long were the nights of aloneness; and who can depart from his pain and his aloneness without regret?

Too many fragments of the spirit have I scattered in these streets, and too many are the children of my longing that walk naked among these hills, and I cannot withdraw from them without a burden and an ache.

It is not a garment I cast off this day, but a skin that I tear with my own hands. Nor is it a thought I leave behind me, but a heart made sweet with hunger and with thirst.

Yet I cannot tarry longer.

The sea that calls all things unto her calls me, and I must embark. For to stay, though the hours burn in the night, is to freeze and crystallize and be bound in a mould.

Fain would I take with me all that is here. But how shall I?

A voice cannot carry the tongue and the lips that give it wings. Alone must it seek the ether. And alone and without his nest shall the eagle fly across the sun.

Now when he reached the foot of the hill, he turned again towards the sea, and he saw his ship approaching the harbour, and upon her prow the mariners, the men of his own land.

他的心靈對他們高唱：

我先人的子孫，浪濤的騎士，你們曾多次在我夢中航行。

而今，在我甦醒時你們翩然來到，這是我更深沉的夢境。

我已準備好離去，我的渴望早已漲滿船帆，等待風起。

只要在這沉靜的氣氛中再吸一口氣，只要朝身後再投注愛戀的一瞥，我就加入你們，成為水手的一員。

而你，廣袤的大海，沉睡的母親。

河流與溪澗唯有奔向你才能感到安詳與自由。

只要小溪再蜿蜒一回，林間再低吟一曲，我就能奔向你，就像一滴無拘無束的水滴，奔回無垠的大海。

他走著，看到遠處的男男女女，從田地和葡萄園快步奔向城門。他聽到他們喊他的名字，在田野間傳佈他的船抵達的消息。

於是他對自己說：

離別之日莫非就是重聚之日？

離別前夕實際上就是我的黎明？

對於這些把犁留在耕地上或是停止榨葡萄汁的人，我該給他們什麼呢？

我的心該變成一棵結實纍纍的果樹，讓我採擷果實，分送給他們嗎？我的願望該如泉湧，注滿他們的杯嗎？

我是否是一座豎琴，可以讓全能的手來撩撥，或是一支長笛，可以任由祂的氣息吹掠？

And his soul cried out to them, and he said:

Sons of my ancient mother, you riders of the tides,

How often have you sailed in my dreams. And now you come in my awakening, which is my deeper dream. Ready am I to go, and my eagerness with sails full set awaits the wind.

Only another breath will I breathe in this still air, only another loving look cast backward, then I shall stand among you, a seafarer among seafarers. And you, vast sea, sleepless mother, Who alone are peace and freedom to the river and the stream, only another winding will this stream make, only another murmur in this glade, And then shall I come to you, a boundless drop to a boundless ocean.

And as he walked he saw from afar men and women leaving their fields and their vineyards and hastening towards the city gates.

And he heard their voices calling his name, and shouting from the field to field telling one another of the coming of the ship.

And he said to himself:

Shall the day of parting be the day of gathering?

And shall it be said that my eve was in truth my dawn?

And what shall I give unto him who has left his plough in midfurrow, or to him who has stopped the wheel of his winepress?

Shall my heart become a tree heavy-laden with fruit that I may gather and give unto them? And shall my desires flow like a fountain that I may fill their cups?

Am I a harp that the hand of the mighty may touch me, or a flute that his breath may pass through me?

船來了

　　我是靜寂的追尋者，而在靜寂中我可曾尋獲什麼珍寶，確信可以分送予人？若說這是我的豐收日，那我又是在哪個不復記憶的季節、哪塊田地上播了種呢？若說這確是我該高懸燈籠之時，那麼燃燒其中的火焰應當不是我的。

　　我舉起的燈籠是空虛而黑暗的，

　　夜的守護者將會為它注滿燈油，把火點亮。

　　他開口述說這些，然而心裏卻有更多話沒有說，只因他無法說出自己深層的秘密。

　　他一進城，眾人就湧向他，齊聲向他呼喊。

　　城中的長者走向前，說道：請先別離開我們。

　　你是我們薄暮時的午陽，你的青春讓我們有了夢想。

　　你絕非陌生人，也不是過客，而是我們的子弟，我們摯愛的人。請不要讓我們的眼睛因渴望見你而痠痛。

　　男祭司和女祭司對他說：

　　現在，不要讓海潮將我們隔開，使得你和我們共度過的時光盡成追憶。你的精神向來與我們同行，你的身影是我們臉上閃爍的光。我們是如此地愛你，然而，我們的愛是蒙著面紗的無言之愛。而現在，這原本無言愛在你面前呼喊出聲，而且願意在你面前展現。

　　愛的體認，只有在別離之際才知其深。

A seeker of silences am I, and what treasure have I found in silences that I may dispense with confidence? If this is my day of harvest, in what fields have I sowed the seed, and in what unremembered seasons? If this indeed be the our in which I lift up my lantern, it is not my flame that shall burn therein.

Empty and dark shall I raise my lantern, and the guardian of the night shall fill it with oil and he shall light it also.

These things he said in words. But much in his heart remained unsaid. For he himself could not speak his deeper secret.

And when he entered into the city all the people came to meet him, and they were crying out to him as with one voice.

And the elders of the city stood forth and said:

Go not yet away from us.

A noontide have you been in our twilight, and your youth has given us dreams to dream.

No stranger are you among us, nor a guest, but our son and our dearly beloved. Suffer not yet our eyes to hunger for your face.

And the priests and the priestesses said unto him:

Let not the waves of the sea separate us now, and the years you have spent in our midst become a memory. You have walked among us a spirit, and your shadow has been a light upon our faces. Much have we loved you. But speechless was our love, and with veils has it been veiled. Yet now it cries aloud unto you, and would stand revealed before you.

And ever has it been that love knows not its own depth until the hour of separation.

其他人也來求他。但他並不回答，僅垂下頭；近旁的人看見他晶瑩的淚珠滑落在胸前。

他和人潮一起走向廟前的大廣場。

此時，神殿中走出一個名叫艾蜜特拉的女預言家。

他極其溫柔地看著她，因為在他進城的第一天，此女子即來找他，並相信了他。

她歡呼祝賀道：

神的預言家，至高真理的探索者，為了尋找你的船，你已經走了很長的路。如今，船已駛近，你必得離去。

對於記憶中的大地和殷盼的居所，你是如此地渴慕；我們的愛不能牽絆你，我們的需要也不能留住你。

我們只求你在離開之前，將真理昭示大眾。

而後，我們可將真理傳給我們的子女，再傳至子孫萬代，永不滅失。

你曾在孤獨中守護我們的時日，在清醒時傾聽我們睡眠中的悲泣與歡笑。現在，就教我們認清自己的面目，並將你在生死之間領悟的一切告訴我們。

他答道：

奧菲里斯城的人哪，除了此刻在你們心神湧現的念頭，我沒別的好說了。

And others came also and entreated him.

But he answered them not. He only bent his head; and those who stood near saw his tears falling upon his breast.

And he and the people proceeded towards the great square before the temple. And there came out of the sanctuary a woman whose name was Almitra. And she was a seeress.

And he looked upon her with exceeding tenderness, for it was she who had first sought and believed in him when he had been but a day in their city.

And she hailed him, saying:

Prophet of God, in quest for the uttermost, long have you searched the distances for your ship. And now your ship has come, and you must needs go. Deep is your longing for the land of your memories and the dwelling place of your greater desires; and our love would not bind you nor our needs hold you.

Yet this we ask ere you leave us, that you speak to us and give us of your truth. And we will give it unto our children, and they unto their children, and it shall not perish.

In your aloneness you have watched with our days, and in your wakefulness you have listened to the weeping and the laughter of our sleep. Now therefore disclose us to ourselves, and tell us all that has been shown you of that which is between birth and death.

And he answered;

People of Orphalese, of what can I speak save of that which is even now moving your souls?

02
愛

於是，艾蜜特拉說，跟我們說說「愛」吧。

他抬起頭，看著眾人，四周一片寂靜。

他大聲說道：

當愛召喚你時，緊隨它，雖然它的道路艱險崎嶇。

當愛的羽翼擁抱你時，依順它，雖然它翅端所藏的尖刺可能會弄傷你。

當愛開口對你說話時，相信它，雖然它的聲音會像北風傾摧花園似地震碎你的夢想。

Then said Almitra, "Speak to us of Love."

And he raised his head and looked upon the people, and there fell a stillness upon them. And with a great voice he said:

When love beckons to you follow him, Though his ways are hard and steep.

And when his wings enfold you yield to him, Though the sword hidden among his pinions may wound you.

And when he speaks to you believe in him, Though his voice may shatter your dreams as the north wind lays waste the garden.

因為，愛既加冕於你，也必把你釘上十字架；愛既使你成長，也必令你受管教。

愛既上升到枝頭，撫慰著你在日光下顫動的嫩葉，也必下潛至根部，搖撼你緊抓住泥土的根節。

愛採集你們，如同農人收割一束束稻穀。

愛像打穀似地鞭出赤裸的你。

愛像篩子似地篩掉你的外穀。

愛像石磨似地磨出你的潔白。

愛更揉捏你使你柔和溫順；

而後，它把你放進神聖的火焰中，使你成為神的聖餐中的聖餅。

這些都是愛會對你做的事，使你洞悉自己內心的秘密，因著這樣的知識，成為「生命本質」的片斷。

然而，如果你因為恐懼，而只求愛的平安和逸樂，

那倒不如遮住自己的赤裸，閃避愛的舂打，

躲進那四季不分、笑不能盡興、哭不能盡情的世界。

For even as love crowns you so shall he crucify you..
Even as he is for your growth so is he for your pruning.

Even as he ascends to your height and caresses your tenderest branches that quiver in the sun, so shall he descend to your roots and shake them in their clinging to the earth.

Like sheaves of corn he gathers you unto himself.
He threshes you to make you naked.
He sifts you to free you from your husks.
He grinds you to whiteness.
He kneads you until you are pliant;
And then he assigns you to his sacred fire, that you may become sacred bread for God's sacred feast.

All these things shall love do unto you that you may know the secrets of your heart, and in that knowledge become a fragment of Life's heart.

But if in your fear you would seek only love's peace and love's pleasure, then it is better for you that you cover your nakedness and pass out of love's threshing-floor, into the seasonless world where you shall laugh, but not all of your laughter, and weep, but not all of your tears.

愛

愛，只付出自己，只拿取自己；

愛，不是佔有，也不是被佔有；

因為，在愛裏一切都得豐足。

　　你付出愛時，不要說「神在我心中」，應當說「我在神心中」。而且，不要以為你可以為愛帶路，因為，愛若覺得你夠資格，它自會為你帶路。

　　愛除了成就自己之外，別無他求。

　　倘若你除了愛還必須有欲，那就欲求這些事吧：

　　融化自己，如同潺潺細流，對著夜晚歡唱，

　　去了解太多溫柔所引起的痛苦。

　　你會因為愛的體認而受傷；

　　並且順服歡欣地讓鮮血流淌。

　　黎明時以雀躍的心醒來，感謝又有一天可以去愛；

　　午間休息時，冥想愛的狂喜；

　　傍晚回家時，滿懷感恩的心；

　　在心中為你摯愛的人祈禱，在你雙唇吟頌讚美詩歌之後，隨即安睡。

Love gives naught but itself and takes naught but from itself.

Love possesses not nor would it be possessed; For love is sufficient unto love.

When you love you should not say, "God is in my heart," but rather, I am in the heart of God." And think not you can direct the course of love, if it finds you worthy, directs your course.

Love has no other desire but to fulfill itself.

But if you love and must needs have desires, let these be your desires:

To melt and be like a running brook that sings its melody to the night.

To know the pain of too much tenderness.

To be wounded by your own understanding of love;

And to bleed willingly and joyfully.

To wake at dawn with a winged heart and give thanks for another day of loving;

To rest at the noon hour and meditate love's ecstasy;

To return home at eventide with gratitude;

And then to sleep with a prayer for the beloved in your heart and a song of praise upon your lips.

03
婚姻

艾蜜特拉再度開口說，那「婚姻」又是什麼呢？

於是，他答道：

你們一同出生，也將長相廝守。

Then Almitra spoke again and said,

　"And what of Marriage, master?"

And he answered saying:

You were born together, and together you shall be forevermore.

婚姻

當死神的羽翼驅散了你們的生命，你們仍將同在。
即使在神靜默的記憶裏，你們也將永遠相守。
但是請在你們相依的世界中保留些許空間，
好讓天堂的風在你們之間舞動。

彼此相愛，但不要使愛成為枷鎖：
讓愛像在你們倆靈魂的岸邊流動的海水。
應當注滿彼此的杯，而不是同飲一杯。
要將自己的麵包給對方，而不是共吃一塊。
兩人一同歌唱、舞蹈，同享歡愉，但仍應保有自我，就像琴
上的弦雖為同一旋律振動，卻仍各自獨立。

奉獻出你們的心，但不要交由對方保管。
因為唯有生命之手才能包容你們的心。
你們要站在一起，但不要靠得太近：
因為廊柱分立才能撐起神殿，
橡樹和柏樹絕無法在彼此的蔭影下成長。

You shall be together when white wings of death scatter your days.

Aye, you shall be together even in the silent memory of God.

But let there be spaces in your togetherness,

And let the winds of the heavens dance between you.

Love one another but make not a bond of love:

Let it rather be a moving sea between the shores of your souls. Fill each other's cup but drink not from one cup. Give one another of your bread but eat not from the same loaf.

Sing and dance together and be joyous, but let each one of you be alone, even as the strings of a lute are alone though they quiver with the same music.

Give your hearts, but not into each other's keeping.

For only the hand of Life can contain your hearts.

And stand together, yet not too near together:

For the pillars of the temple stand apart,

And the oak tree and the cypress grow not in each other's shadow.

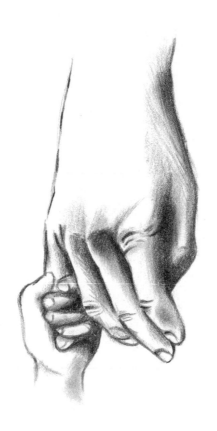

04
孩子

一位抱著嬰兒的婦女說，請和我們說說「孩子」。

他於是說道：

你的孩子不是你的孩子。

And a woman who held a babe against her bosom said,
  "Speak to us of Children."

And he said:

Your children are not your children.

孩子

他們是生命渴求的兒女，是生命本身的企盼。
他們只是藉由你而生，並非為你而來，
他們會與你同在，卻不附屬於你。

你可以給予他們你的愛，而不是思想，
因為他們有自己的思想。
你可以給予他們安居之處，卻不能禁錮他們的靈魂，
因為他們的靈魂棲身在明日之屋，
你不僅無法探訪，甚至不在你的夢想裡。
你可以努力揣摩他們，但不要想像他們與你相同。
生命無法倒流，也不會停滯於昨日。

你是弓，孩子如生命的箭經由你射向前方。
弓箭手看見無盡路途中的目標，便用祂的力氣將你這把弓彎
曲，希望這支箭射得又快又遠。
愉悅地屈服於弓箭手的作為吧；
因為他不僅愛飛馳的箭，也愛穩固的弓。

On Children

They are the sons and daughters of Life's longing for itself.

They come through you but not from you,

And though they are with you, yet they belong not to you.

You may give them your love but not your thoughts.

For they have their own thoughts.

You may house their bodies but not their souls,

For their souls dwell in the house of tomorrow, which you cannot visit, not even in your dreams.

You may strive to be like them, but seek not to make them like you.For life goes not backward nor tarries with yesterday.

You are the bows from which your children as living arrows are sent forth.

The archer sees the mark upon the path of the infinite, and He bends you with His might that His arrows may go swift and far.

Let your bending in the archer's hand be for gladness;

For even as he loves the arrow that flies, so He loves also the bow that is stable.

05
給予

一個富人說，跟我們說說「給予」吧。

他於是答道：

你把財產給人時，你給得很少，

你若是將自己獻上，才是真正的「給予」。

Then said a rich man, "Speak to us of Giving."

And he answered:

You give but little when you give of your possessions.

It is when you give of yourself that you truly give.

財產只是你害怕明日會需要而儲備的東西吧？

然而明天，明天會帶給一隻思慮過慎的狗什麼呢？牠隨著朝聖者去聖城，在途中把骨頭埋在無跡可尋的沙裏。

需要的恐懼是什麼？不就是需要本身嗎？

若井水滿溢時，你仍害怕會口渴，那麼，你的渴豈不是無法消解？

有些人擁有很多，卻給得很少——而且是為了沽名釣譽。他們隱藏的欲望使得拿出來的禮物失去價值。

也有人擁有的不多，卻樂於全部獻出。

這樣的人相信生命本身是豐厚富足的，他們的寶庫永遠不會空乏。

有人歡欣地給予，而歡欣便是他們的報酬。

有人痛苦地給予，而痛苦便是他們的洗禮。

也有人只是單純地給予，既不覺得痛苦也不因之歡喜，更不為彰顯自己的品德；

他們的給予，就像遠處山谷裏的桃金孃，讓空氣飄逸著清香。神藉著他們的手傳講祂的話語，經由他們的眼對大地微笑。

For what are your possessions but things you keep and guard for fear you may need them tomorrow?

And tomorrow, what shall tomorrow bring to the overprudent dog burying bones in the trackless sand as he follows the pilgrims to the holy city?

And what is fear of need but need itself?

Is not dread of thirst when your well is full, thirst that is unquenchable?

There are those who give little of the much which they have -- and they give it for recognition and their hidden desire makes their gifts unwholesome.

And there are those who have little and give it all.

These are the believers in life and the bounty of life, and their coffer is never empty.

There are those who give with joy, and that joy is their reward.

And there are those who give with pain, and that pain is their baptism.

And there are those who give and know not pain in giving, nor do they seek joy, nor give with mindfulness of virtue;

They give as in yonder valley the myrtle breathes its fragrance into space. Though the hands of such as these God speaks, and from behind their eyes He smiles upon the earth.

在他人求助時給予誠屬好事，然而，在他人未開口之前即體貼地付出更好；對於樂善好施的人來說，尋找施予的對象比施予本身的喜樂更大。

你有什麼東西不想給人嗎？你所擁有的一切終將要讓出來；因此，現在就給吧，趁著給予的時節還屬於你，而不是你的後人。

你常說：「我願意給，但是只給受之無愧的人。」

然而，你果園裏的樹不這麼說，你牧場上的羊也不這麼說。

他們因為給予才能延續生命，保留而不給會走向滅亡。

凡是值得神賜予白晝和黑夜的人，當然也值得你給予的一切。凡是有資格從生命海洋取水來喝的人，當然也配從你的小溪取水注滿他的杯。還有什麼比接受施捨的勇氣和信心——姑且不談慈悲——更大的美德？

而你是誰？為何人們得在你面前袒露胸懷，揭開自尊，好讓你看到他們赤裸的價值和無愧的自尊？先審視你自己是否夠資格成為施予者，是否能成為神施予的器皿。

事實上，只有生命才能給予生命，而自認是施予者的你，不過是個見證人罷了。

至於你們這些受施者——你們全都是受施者——不要有感激的重擔，否則就是將頸箍架在自己和施予者的頸項上了。

不如以施予者的禮物為羽翼，和他一同飛昇；因為，過於記掛你的負欠，就是懷疑施予者的慷慨，懷疑那以恢弘的大地為母親、全能的神為父親的施予者。

It is well to give when asked, but it is better to give unasked, through understanding; And to the open-handed the search for one who shall receive is joy greater than giving.

And is there aught you would withhold? All you have shall some day be given; Therefore give now, that the season of giving may be yours and not your inheritors'.

You often say, "I would give, but only to the deserving."

The trees in your orchard say not so, nor the flocks in your pasture. They give that they may live, for to withhold is to perish. Surely he who is worthy to receive his days and his nights is worthy of all else from you. And he who has deserved to drink from the ocean of life deserves to fill his cup from your little stream.

And what desert greater shall there be than that which lies in the courage and the confidence, nay the charity, of receiving?

And who are you that men should rend their bosom and unveil their pride, that you may see their worth naked and their pride unabashed? See first that you yourself deserve to be a giver, and an instrument of giving.

For in truth it is life that gives unto life -- while you, who deem yourself a giver, are but a witness.

And you receivers -- and you are all receivers -- assume no weight of gratitude, lest you lay a yoke upon yourself and upon him who gives.

Rather rise together with the giver on his gifts as on wings; For to be overmindful of your debt, is to doubt his generosity who has the free-hearted earth for mother, and God for father.

06
飲食

一個老人，一家客棧的老闆說，和我們談談「飲食」吧。

於是他回答道：

但願你們能靠大地的芬芳而活，就像植物一樣，有陽光就能維生。

Then an old man, a keeper of an inn, said,

　"Speak to us of Eating and Drinking."

And he said:

Would that you could live on the fragrance of the earth, and like an air plant be sustained by the light.

　　但是，既然你們必須因食而殺生，並且從新生動物的口中奪取奶水來止渴，那就讓這事成為一種敬拜行為。

　　讓你的餐桌成為祭壇，其上擺的是來自林野中純潔無瑕的生命，它們是人心中更純潔更無瑕的牲禮。

　　當你宰殺一隻野獸時，在心裏對牠說：

　　「宰殺你的力量也必宰殺我，我也將會被吞食。

　　將你交到我手裏的法則，也必將我交到更強者之手。

　　你我的血都不過是澆灌天堂樹木的汁液。」

　　當你用牙齒啃吃蘋果時，在心裏對它說：

　　「你的種子將活在我體內，

　　你明日的芽苞將在我心中綻放，

　　你芬芳的香味將是我的氣息，

　　我們將歡喜地共度所有的季節。」

　　秋天，當你在葡萄園採集葡萄準備釀酒時，在心裏說道：

　　「我亦是一座葡萄園，我的果實也會被採去釀酒，

　　如同新釀的酒一樣，我會被保存在永恆的器皿中。」

　　冬天，當你斟酒時，在心中對每杯酒都唱首歌吧；

　　在歌中唱出對秋日、對葡萄園和榨酒機的回憶。

But since you must kill to eat, and rob the young of its mother's milk to quench your thirst, let it then be an act of worship,

And let your board stand an altar on which the pure and the innocent of forest and plain are sacrificed for that which is purer and still more innocent in many.

When you kill a beast say to him in your heart,

"By the same power that slays you, I to am slain; and I too shall be consumed. For the law that delivered you into my hand shall deliver me into a mightier hand. Your blood and my blood is naught but the sap that feeds the tree of heaven."

And when you crush an apple with your teeth, say to it in your heart, "Your seeds shall live in my body, And the buds of your tomorrow shall blossom in my heart, And your fragrance shall be my breath, And together we shall rejoice through all the seasons."

And in the autumn, when you gather the grapes of your vineyard for the winepress, say in you heart,

"I to am a vineyard, and my fruit shall be gathered for the winepress, And like new wine I shall be kept in eternal vessels."

And in winter, when you draw the wine, let there be in your heart a song for each cup;

And let there be in the song a remembrance for the autumn days, and for the vineyard, and for the winepress.

07
工作

一個農夫說，跟我們談談「工作」吧。

於是他答道：

工作可以使你跟上世界的腳步，緊隨世界的靈魂。

因為遊手好閒會使你成為歲月的陌生人，使你脫離正莊嚴及光榮服從地邁向永恆的生命隊伍。

在工作時，你彷如一支長笛，時間的呢喃透過它轉變成音樂。

當天地萬物和諧地奏出樂聲，你們誰願意當一支黯啞、沉默的蘆葦呢？

Then a ploughman said, "Speak to us of Work."

And he answered, saying:

You work that you may keep pace with the earth and the soul of the earth.

For to be idle is to become a stranger unto the seasons, and to step out of life's procession, that marches in majesty and proud submission towards the infinite.

When you work you are a flute through whose heart the whispering of the hours turns to music. Which of you would be a reed, dumb and silent, when all else sings together in unison?

　　總有人告訴你，工作是個咒詛，勞動更是不幸。

　　但是我告訴你，當你工作時，就實現了一部分大地最深遠的夢，而這個夢在誕生時就已指派給你。

　　況且，勞動不息的你才是真正熱愛生命，

　　透過勞動來愛生命，也就是親近生命最深層的秘密。

　　然而，若你在痛苦中宣稱誕生是一種磨難，肉體的維生是寫在你眉宇間的詛咒，那麼我說，唯有你眉間滴下的汗水，才能拭去上頭的載記。

　　也有人告訴你，生命乃是一片黑暗，而你在疲乏時，也就隨聲附和那些疲乏的人。

　　然而我說，生命的確是黑暗，除非有盼望，

　　所有盼望都是盲目，除非有知識，

　　所有知識都是枉然，除非有工作，

　　所有工作都是虛空，除非愛在其中；

　　你若懷著愛工作，就會讓自己和他人以及神結合在一起。

　　什麼是懷著愛來工作呢？

　　就是以你心中抽出的絲線來織布，彷彿這屋宇是你摯愛的人要住的。就是溫柔地撒種，喜悅地收割，彷彿收得的果實是你摯愛的人要享用的。就是用你的精神在所有事情上注入你的風格，並且知道，所有蒙祝福的故人都站在你的四周觀望著。

Always you have been told that work is a curse and labour a misfortune. But I say to you that when you work you fulfil a part of earth's furthest dream, assigned to you when that dream was born, and in keeping yourself with labour you are in truth loving life, and to love life through labour is to be intimate with life's inmost secret.

But if you in your pain call birth an affliction and the support of the flesh a curse written upon your brow, then I answer that naught but the sweat of your brow shall wash away that which is written.

You have been told also life is darkness, and in your weariness you echo what was said by the weary.

And I say that life is indeed darkness save when there is urge,

And all urge is blind save when there is knowledge,

And all knowledge is vain save when there is work,

And all work is empty save when there is love;

And when you work with love you bind yourself to yourself, and to one another, and to God.

And what is it to work with love?

It is to weave the cloth with threads drawn from your heart, even as if your beloved were to wear that cloth.

It is to build a house with affection, even as if your beloved were to dwell in that house. It is to sow seeds with tenderness and reap the harvest with joy, even as if your beloved were to eat the fruit. It is to charge all things you fashion with a breath of your own spirit, and to know that all the blessed dead are standing about you and watching.

工作

　　我常聽你們夢囈似地說著：「那雕刻大理石，而且在其中展現自己靈魂的人，比在田裏耕種的人高貴。那抓住彩虹，用它在布帛上畫出人形的人，比為我們製作涼鞋的人了不起。」

　　但是，在這正午時分，不是在睡夢中，我神智清醒地告訴你們，風對巨大橡樹說的話，不會比對微小葉片說的話甜蜜；

　　惟有能用愛將風的話變成甜蜜歌聲的人，才堪稱高貴偉大。

　　工作是愛的具體表現，

　　若你無法懷著愛來工作，反而心懷厭惡，那麼你最好辭掉工作，坐在寺廟的大門口，接受樂在工作的人給你的施捨。

　　因為，你若是冷漠地烘烤麵包，就會烤出只能讓人半飽的苦麵包。

　　若你怨懟地釀榨葡萄酒，你將把酒釀成毒藥。

　　若你雖有天使般的歌聲，卻不愛歌唱，你就是搗住了人耳，使他聽不見白天和夜晚的聲音。

Often have I heard you say, as if speaking in sleep, "he who works in marble, and finds the shape of his own soul in the stone, is a nobler than he who ploughs the soil.

And he who seizes the rainbow to lay it on a cloth in the likeness of man, is more than he who makes the sandals for our feet."

But I say, not in sleep but in the over--wakefulness of noontide, that the wind speaks not more sweetly to the giant oaks than to the least of all the blades of grass;

And he alone is great who turns the voice of the wind into a song made sweeter by his own loving.

Work is love made visible.

And if you cannot work with love but only with distaste, it is better that you should leave your work and sit at the gate of the temple and take alms of those who work with joy.

For if you bake bread with indifference, you bake a bitter bread that feeds but half man's hunger.

And if you grudge the crushing of the grapes, your grudge distils a poison in the wine.

And if you sing though as angels, and love not the singing, you muffle man's ears to the voices of the day and the voices of the night.

08
歡樂與悲傷

一個婦人說，請談談「歡樂」和「悲傷」吧。

他答道：

你的歡樂是未加掩飾的悲傷。

湧出歡樂的那口井，通常也裝滿了你的淚水。

Then a woman said, "Speak to us of Joy and Sorrow."

And he answered:

Your joy is your sorrow unmasked.

And the selfsame well from which your laughter rises was oftentimes filled with your tears.

怎麼可能會有別的情況？

悲傷在你身上雕刻的痕跡愈深，你所能盛裝的歡樂就愈多。

你用來盛酒的杯子，不是曾在陶匠的窯裏燒過嗎？

那撫慰你精神的琴，不就是那塊用刀鑿過的木頭嗎？

當你歡樂時，看著自己的內心深處，你會發覺，現時的快樂乃源於之前經歷過的悲傷。

當你悲傷時，再次看著內心深處，你會發覺你是在為以前的歡樂哭泣。有人說，「歡樂大於悲傷，」也有人說，「不，悲傷才是更大的。」

但是我要告訴你們，這兩者是永不分離的。

它們一同來到，當其中一個坐在你的桌邊時，切記，另一個正在你的床上安歇。

事實上，你就像是在歡樂和悲傷間擺盪的天秤。

唯有心中空無一念時，才可平衡靜止。

當看守財物的人拿你去秤金量銀，你的歡樂或悲傷必然會跟著起起落落。

And how else can it be?

The deeper that sorrow carves into your being, the more joy you can contain.

Is not the cup that hold your wine the very cup that was burned in the potter's oven?

And is not the lute that soothes your spirit, the very wood that was hollowed with knives?

When you are joyous, look deep into your heart and you shall find it is only that which has given you sorrow that is giving you joy.

When you are sorrowful look again in your heart, and you shall see that in truth you are weeping for that which has been your delight. Some of you say, "Joy is greater than sorrow," and others say, "Nay, sorrow is the greater."

But I say unto you, they are inseparable.

Together they come, and when one sits alone with you at your board, remember that the other is asleep upon your bed.

Verily you are suspended like scales between your sorrow and your joy.

Only when you are empty are you at standstill and balanced.

When the treasure-keeper lifts you to weigh his gold and his silver, needs must your joy or your sorrow rise or fall.

09
房屋

一個泥水匠走過來說，請跟我們談談「房屋」吧。

他回答道：

你在城裏蓋一棟房屋之前，先用想像力在曠野中建造一座涼亭。

因為，正如你會在薄暮時返家，你心中那個向來遙遠而孤單的流浪者也將回來。

你的屋宇乃是你身體的延伸。

Then a mason came forth and said,

"Speak to us of Houses."

And he answered and said:

Build of your imaginings a bower in the wilderness ere you build a house within the city walls.

For even as you have home-comings in your twilight, so has the wanderer in you, the ever distant and alone.

Your house is your larger body.

房屋

它在陽光下成長，在夜的寂靜中歇息；它並非無夢。難道你的屋宇不作夢嗎？它不正夢想著離開城市到樹林或山頂上去嗎？

多麼希望我能將你們的屋宇全收在手裏，然後撒種似的將它們撒在森林和草地上。

但願山谷是你們的街道，綠徑是你們的小巷，你們穿過葡萄園互相尋訪，回來時衣上沾著泥土的芬芳。

然而這些都尚未實現。

你們的祖先因恐懼而讓你們緊挨在一起，這樣的恐懼仍會持續一段時間。你們的屋舍與田野仍將暫時為城牆所分隔。

奧菲里斯城的居民，請告訴我，你們的屋裏有什麼呢？你們緊閉門扉守護著什麼呢？

你們有平靜嗎？那讓你們顯出力量的沉靜驅力？

你們有回憶嗎？那座跨越心靈頂端的閃耀拱門？

你們有美嗎？那引領心靈從木石製品走向聖山的美？

告訴我，你們的房屋裏有這些東西嗎？

或者，你們有的只是舒適，以及對舒適的慾望？那鬼祟地進入你家，以賓客身分逐漸爬上主人地位的東西。

It grows in the sun and sleeps in the stillness of the night; and it is not dreamless. Does not your house dream? And dreaming, leave the city for grove or hilltop?

Would that I could gather your houses into my hand, and like a sower scatter them in forest and meadow.

Would the valleys were your streets, and the green paths your alleys, that you might seek one another through vineyards, and come with the fragrance of the earth in your garments.

But these things are not yet to be.

In their fear your forefathers gathered you too near together. And that fear shall endure a little longer. A little longer shall your city walls separate your hearths from your fields.

And tell me, people of Orphalese, what have you in these houses? And what is it you guard with fastened doors?

Have you peace, the quiet urge that reveals your power?

Have you remembrances, the glimmering arches that span the summits of the mind?

Have you beauty, that leads the heart from things fashioned of wood and stone to the holy mountain?

Tell me, have you these in your houses?

Or have you only comfort, and the lust for comfort, that stealthy thing that enters the house a guest, and becomes a host, and then a master?

　　哎！它變成了馴獸師，以鐵鉤和鞭子把你更大的慾望馴成傀儡。

　　雖然它的手柔滑如絲，它的心卻剛硬如鐵。

　　它哄你入睡，只為站在床側譏諷人類的尊嚴。

　　它嘲笑你清明的神智，將之視為易碎的器皿置放於絨毛上。

　　的確，對舒適的慾望會扼殺性靈的熱情，而在葬禮時獰笑著走過。

　　但是你們，蒼穹的兒女，在歇息中仍保持警醒，就不會被誘捕，也不會被馴服。

　　你們的屋宇不是錨而是桅杆。

　　它不是遮蔽傷口的閃亮薄膜，而是護衛眼睛的眼瞼。

　　不要為穿越屋門而收起雙翼，不要為怕撞到天花板而畏縮著頭，更不要怕牆垣坍塌而屏住呼吸。

　　你不該住在死人為生者所築的墳墓中。

　　儘管你的屋宇富麗雄偉、金碧輝煌，它也不該藏起你的秘密，遮蔽你的渴望。

　　因為你無窮的心居住在蒼穹的華廈中，它以晨霧為門，以夜的詩歌和靜謐為窗。

Ay, and it becomes a tamer, and with hook and scourge makes puppets of your larger desires.

Though its hands are silken, its heart is of iron.

It lulls you to sleep only to stand by your bed and jeer at the dignity of the flesh. It makes mock of your sound senses, and lays them in thistledown like fragile vessels.

Verily the lust for comfort murders the passion of the soul, and then walks grinning in the funeral.

But you, children of space, you restless in rest, you shall not be trapped nor tamed.

Your house shall be not an anchor but a mast.

It shall not be a glistening film that covers a wound, but an eyelid that guards the eye.

You shall not fold your wings that you may pass through doors, nor bend your heads that they strike not against a ceiling, nor fear to breathe lest walls should crack and fall down.

You shall not dwell in tombs made by the dead for the living.

And though of magnificence and splendour, your house shall not hold your secret nor shelter your longing.

For that which is boundless in you abides in the mansion of the sky, whose door is the morning mist, and whose windows are the songs and the silences of night.

10
衣服

一個織工說，請和我們談談「衣服」吧。

於是他答道：

衣服遮掩了你們許多的美，卻遮不住醜。

And the weaver said, "Speak to us of Clothes."

And he answered:

Your clothes conceal much of your beauty, yet they hide not the unbeautiful.

衣服

　雖然你想在衣裝中尋求隱密的自由，卻反而在其中發現束縛和捆鎖。

　但願你多用肌膚迎向煦日和風，而少用衣服。

　因為生命的氣息在日光裏，生命的手在風中。

　有人說，「是北風織了我們穿的衣服。」

　我說，是啊，的確是北風織的，

　但是，羞恥是它的機杼，柔軟的肌肉是它的絲線。

　它做完工作時，就在森林裏大笑。

　不要忘了，端莊是擋遮不潔之眼的盾牌。

　當不潔之眼不復存在時，端莊豈不成了心上的束縛和阻礙嗎？

　不要忘了，大地喜歡撫觸你赤裸的雙足，風更期盼與你的秀髮嬉戲。

On Clothes

And though you seek in garments the freedom of privacy you may find in them a harness and a chain.

Would that you could meet the sun and the wind with more of your skin and less of your raiment,

For the breath of life is in the sunlight and the hand of life is in the wind.

Some of you say, "It is the north wind who has woven the clothes to wear."

And I say, Aye, it was the north wind,

But shame was his loom, and the softening of the sinews was his thread.

And when his work was done he laughed in the forest.

Forget not that modesty is for a shield against the eye of the unclean.

And when the unclean shall be no more, what were modesty but a fetter and a fouling of the mind?

And forget not that the earth delights to feel your bare feet and the winds long to play with your hair.

11
買賣

一個商人說，跟我們談談「買賣」吧。

他回答道：

大地賜給你們果實，只要你們懂得盛滿雙手，就不致於匱乏。

And a merchant said, "Speak to us of Buying and Selling."

And he answered and said:

To you the earth yields her fruit, and you shall not want if you but know how to fill your hands.

在和大地交換禮物時，必因其豐富而得滿足。

然而，這交換若不是憑藉愛和仁慈的公義，就會使一些人貪婪，使另外一些人挨餓。

在市場上，你們這些在海上、田裏和葡萄園中辛苦工作的人，會遇見織布工、陶匠和採集香料的人

你們要召請大地之神降臨，淨化你們量物的天秤，使你們計算物價的方法公平正當。

絕不要讓那手無一物的人介入你們的交易，因為這樣的人只會用口舌之詐換走你所付出的勞力。

你應該對這種人說：

「跟我們到田裏，或是和我們的兄弟到海上，撒下你的網；因為土地和海洋會賜給你富足，就像對我們一樣。」

如果市集上來了歌者、舞者和吹笛人——也要去購買他們天賦的贈禮。

因為這些人也是果實和乳香的採集者，雖然他們提拱的如夢似幻，卻是你們靈魂的衣服和食物。

離開市場之前，你們要確認沒有人空手而回。

因為，大地之神必須滿足每個人最起碼的需求之後，才會安心地在風中歇息

It is in exchanging the gifts of the earth that you shall find abundance and be satisfied.

Yet unless the exchange be in love and kindly justice, it will but lead some to greed and others to hunger.

When in the market place you toilers of the sea and fields and vineyards meet the weavers and the potters and the gatherers of spices, invoke then the master spirit of the earth, to come into your midst and sanctify the scales and the reckoning that weighs value against value.

And suffer not the barren-handed to take part in your transactions, who would sell their words for your labour.

To such men you should say,

"Come with us to the field, or go with our brothers to the sea and cast your net; For the land and the sea shall be bountiful to you even as to us."

And if there come the singers and the dancers and the flute players, -- buy of their gifts also. For they too are gatherers of fruit and frankincense, and that which they bring, though fashioned of dreams, is raiment and food for your soul.

And before you leave the marketplace, see that no one has gone his way with empty hands.

For the master spirit of the earth shall not sleep peacefully upon the wind till the needs of the least of you are satisfied.

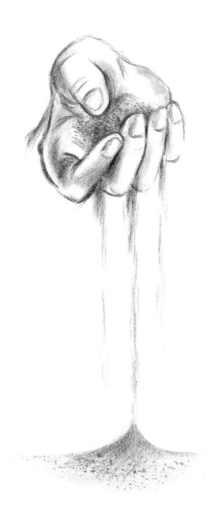

12
罪與罰

城裏一位法官站出來說，請和我們談談「罪與罰」吧。

他答道：

當你的精神隨風飄盪時，孤獨而無防衛的你才會對別人犯錯，也因此對自己犯錯。

為了這個過失，你必須到有福者的門口敲門等候，卻一時無人理睬。

Then one of the judges of the city stood forth and said,

"Speak to us of Crime and Punishment."

And he answered saying:

It is when your spirit goes wandering upon the wind,

That you, alone and unguarded, commit a wrong unto others and therefore unto yourself.

And for that wrong committed must you knock and wait a while unheeded at the gate of the blessed.

你心中的神宛如海洋；

永遠不會被玷污。

也如藍天一樣，只容有翅者翱翔。

你心中的神甚至像太陽；

不知鼴鼠的地道，也不去尋找蛇的洞穴。

然而，在你的心中不只有「神性面」而已。

你的心中有一大部是人，還有一大部分連人都不是，

而只是未成形的侏儒，在迷霧中夢遊，尋求自己的覺醒。

我現在要談的是你心中的那個人。

因為懂得「罪與罰」的，既不是你心中的神，也不是迷霧中的侏儒，而是那個人。

我常聽你們談論某個做錯事的人，彷彿他並非你們的一份子，而是闖進你們世界裏的陌生人。

然而，我卻要說，那些聖潔和公義之人，也無法超越你們任何一人的至善本質，

同樣地，惡人與弱者也不比你們任何一人的低劣本質更沈淪。

Like the ocean is your god-self;

It remains for ever undefiled.

And like the ether it lifts but the winged.

Even like the sun is your god-self;

It knows not the ways of the mole nor seeks it the holes of the serpent.

But your god-self does not dwell alone in your being.

Much in you is still man, and much in you is not yet man,

But a shapeless pigmy that walks asleep in the mist searching for its own awakening.

And of the man in you would I now speak.

For it is he and not your god-self nor the pigmy in the mist, that knows crime and the punishment of crime.

Oftentimes have I heard you speak of one who commits a wrong as though he were not one of you, but a stranger unto you and an intruder upon your world.

But I say that even as the holy and the righteous cannot rise beyond the highest which is in each one of you,

如同一片葉子，沒有整棵樹的默許就不會變黃，

沒有你們隱藏的惡念，犯錯者也不會為惡。

你們就像一支隊伍，一起走向心中的神，

你們本身是道路，也是路上的旅人。

你們之中若有人跌倒，他是為了後排的人跌倒，要他們當心會絆倒人的石頭。

他也是在為前排的人跌倒，因為那些人步伐雖快、步履雖穩，卻沒有將那絆腳石挪開。

還有，雖然這些話會重重地壓在你們的心上，我仍得說：

被謀殺者對自己的遭遇不是全無責任，

被搶之人也不是全無過失。

正人君子對邪惡之徒的行為亦需負責。

清白之人與殘暴之徒的作為也難脫關係。

是的，犯罪者常是受害者的代罪羔羊，

更常見的是，被定罪的人背負著無罪無過者的重擔。

你們無法區分正與邪、善與惡；

因為它們站在一起面對太陽，就像黑線與白線交織在一起。

當黑絲斷了，織工必會察看整塊布，也會檢查織布機。

And as a single leaf turns not yellow but with the silent knowledge of the whole tree, so the wrong-doer cannot do wrong without the hidden will of you all.

Like a procession you walk together towards your god-self.

You are the way and the wayfarers.

And when one of you falls down he falls for those behind him, a caution against the stumbling stone.

Ay, and he falls for those ahead of him, who though faster and surer of foot, yet removed not the stumbling stone.

And this also, though the word lie heavy upon your hearts:

The murdered is not unaccountable for his own murder,

And the robbed is not blameless in being robbed.

The righteous is not innocent of the deeds of the wicked,

And the white-handed is not clean in the doings of the felon.

Yea, the guilty is oftentimes the victim of the injured,

And still more often the condemned is the burden-bearer for the guiltless and unblamed.

You cannot separate the just from the unjust and the good from the wicked; For they stand together before the face of the sun even as the black thread and the white are woven together.

And when the black thread breaks, the weaver shall look into the whole cloth, and he shall examine the loom also.

　　若你們之中有人要審判不忠實的妻子，

　　那麼，請他秤一秤她丈夫的心，量一量她丈夫的靈魂。

　　讓那欲鞭笞罪犯的人先審視受害者的心靈。

　　若你們之中有人要以正義之名懲處別人，並將斧頭砍向惡樹，那麼，讓他看看樹根；他必會發現，善與惡的根、結果實和不結果實的根，全都交纏在大地靜默的心中。

　　而你們這些自稱公正的法官，

　　對於身體誠實但內心欺盜的人，你們要如何宣判？

　　對於那殺人身體但心靈飽受摧殘的人，你們又當如何處罰？

　　對於那欺詐、壓迫別人，本身也遭受迫害而憤憤不平的人，你們如何起訴他呢？

　　還有，對於那些已經因過錯而深自痛悔的人，你們又該如何處罰呢？悔改不就是你們所熱切遵循的法律所伸張的正義嗎？

　　然而，你們不能讓無辜者懺悔，也無法使罪人心中釋然。

　　懺悔將在夜裏不請自來，令人清醒，審視自己的言行。

　　而你們這些了解正義的人，若不能在充足的明光下審視所有的行為，又要如何了解呢？

　　只有在這時候，你們才會明白，那直立的和傾倒的其實是同一人，他就站在侏儒的夜和神的白晝間的朦朧地帶，

　　而且，神殿的房角石並不比它地基中最低的石頭高。

If any of you would bring judgment the unfaithful wife, Let him also weight the heart of her husband in scales, and measure his soul with measurements. And let him who would lash the offender look unto the spirit of the offended.

And if any of you would punish in the name of righteousness and lay the ax unto the evil tree, let him see to its roots;

And verily he will find the roots of the good and the bad, the fruitful and the fruitless, all entwined together in the silent heart of the earth.

And you judges who would be just,

What judgment pronounce you upon him who though honest in the flesh yet is a thief in spirit? What penalty lay you upon him who slays in the flesh yet is himself slain in the spirit? And how prosecute you him who in action is a deceiver and an oppressor, Yet who also is aggrieved and outraged? And how shall you punish those whose remorse is already greater than their misdeeds?

Is not remorse the justice which is administered by that very law which you would fain serve?

Yet you cannot lay remorse upon the innocent nor lift it from the heart of the guilty. Unbidden shall it call in the night, that men may wake and gaze upon themselves. And you who would understand justice, how shall you unless you look upon all deeds in the fullness of light?

Only then shall you know that the erect and the fallen are but one man standing in twilight between the night of his pigmy-self and the day of his god-self, and that the corner-stone of the temple is not higher than the lowest stone in its foundation.

13
法律

一個律師接著問道，那「法律」又是怎樣呢，大師？

他於是答道：

你們極愛立法，卻更愛犯法。

就像孩童在海邊玩耍時，堅定地在沙上築塔，然後又笑著把它毀掉。

但是，築塔時，大海把更多的泥沙送至岸邊，而當你毀掉所築的塔時，大海也和你一起大笑。

確實，大海總是和天真的人一同歡笑。

Then a lawyer said, "But what of our Laws, master?"

And he answered:

You delight in laying down laws,

Yet you delight more in breaking them.

Like children playing by the ocean who build sand-towers with constancy and then destroy them with laughter.

But while you build your sand-towers the ocean brings more sand to the shore, and when you destroy them, the ocean laughs with you.

Verily the ocean laughs always with the innocent.

然而，有些人並不把生命看成海洋，也不把人所制頒的法律看成沙塔，對這些人又該怎麼說呢？

他們認為生命是塊岩石，法律是他們用來在石上雕出自己形像的鑿刀。

對於恨惡舞者的瘸子而言，又該怎麼說？

如果牛喜愛自己的頸軛，認為林中的麋鹿皆為漂泊的流浪漢，那該怎麼說？

老蛇無法蛻皮，卻因此說其他的蛇不知羞恥地赤身裸體，這又該怎麼說？

有人提早赴婚宴，因吃得過於飽足而難以行路，便說所有筵席都違法，全部宴客皆犯紀，對這樣的人又該怎麼說？

對於這些人我能說什麼？只能說他們雖然站在陽光下，卻背對著太陽。

But what of those to whom life is not an ocean, and man-made laws are not sand-towers,

But to whom life is a rock, and the law a chisel with which they would carve it in their own likeness?

What of the cripple who hates dancers?

What of the ox who loves his yoke and deems the elk and deer of the forest stray and vagrant things?

What of the old serpent who cannot shed his skin, and calls all others naked and shameless?

And of him who comes early to the wedding-feast, and when over-fed and tired goes his way saying that all feasts are violation and all feasters law-breakers?

What shall I say of these save that they too stand in the sunlight, but with their backs to the sun?

法律

他們只看到自己的影子，而他們的影子就是法律。

對他們而言，太陽豈不只是投射影子的東西？

承認法律，不就是彎著腰在地上找自己的影子嗎？

然而，若是你們面向太陽行走，豈能被地上的投影羈絆住呢？

你們御風而行，要靠什麼風向標指引？

如果你們打破自己的頸軛，只要不跌倒在別人的牢門，法律豈能綑縛你們呢？

如果你們可以跳舞，只要不絆倒在他人的鐵鍊上，你們又何必害怕法律？

如果你們撕裂自己的外衣而不丟棄在別人的通道上，有誰能押你去接受審判呢？

奧菲里斯城的人哪，你們可以壓低鼓聲，也可以調鬆琴弦，然而，有誰能令雲雀噤聲呢？

They see only their shadows, and their shadows are their laws.

And what is the sun to them but a caster of shadows?

And what is it to acknowledge the laws but to stoop down and trace their shadows upon the earth?

But you who walk facing the sun, what images drawn on the earth can hold you?

You who travel with the wind, what weathervane shall direct your course?

What man's law shall bind you if you break your yoke but upon no man's prison door?

What laws shall you fear if you dance but stumble against no man's iron chains?

And who is he that shall bring you to judgment if you tear off your garment yet leave it in no man's path?

People of Orphalese, you can muffle the drum, and you can loosen the strings of the lyre, but who shall command the skylark not to sing?

14
自由

一個演說家說，跟我們談談「自由」吧。

他於是答道：

在城門前和你們的火爐邊，我看見你們跪地敬拜自己的自由，就像奴隸謙卑地歌頌暴君，儘管終免不了被屠殺。

哎，在神殿的樹叢和城堡的影子下，我看見你們當中最自由的人，將自由如同手銬頸軛一般戴在自己身上。

And an orator said, "Speak to us of Freedom."

And he answered:

At the city gate and by your fireside I have seen you prostrate yourself and worship your own freedom, even as slaves humble themselves before a tyrant and praise him though he slays them.

Ay, in the grove of the temple and in the shadow of the citadel I have seen the freest among you wear their freedom as a yoke and a handcuff.

自由

　　我的內心在淌血；除非你們能體認那追求自己的慾望變成你的韁繩，不把自由說成是要實現的目標時，才能真的自由。

　　真正的自由，並不是在白晝無所牽掛，在黑夜無所冀求、毫無憂傷，乃是在這些事情纏攪你時，你能坦然不受羈絆地超脫出來。除非你能掙脫在你了解到黎明時，已繫上的正午的鎖鍊，否則如何能超越白晝與黑夜呢？

　　事實上，你們所謂的自由是鎖鍊中最強固的一環，只是它在陽光下閃爍耀眼，令你們目眩。

　　你們所要捨棄以尋求自由的，不也是自我的一部分？

　　你們欲廢除的不公正的法律，乃是你親手寫在自己額上的。

　　就算焚毀法律書籍，或以一洋之水沖刷法官的前額，也無法洗去不公正的法律。

　　如果你們想要推翻暴君，首先要確定他在你們內心建立的王位已被摧毀。

On Freedom

And my heart bled within me; for you can only be free when even the desire of seeking freedom becomes a harness to you, and when you cease to speak of freedom as a goal and a fulfillment.

You shall be free indeed when your days are not without a care nor your nights without a want and a grief, but rather when these things girdle your life and yet you rise above them naked and unbound.

And how shall you rise beyond your days and nights unless you break the chains which you at the dawn of your understanding have fastened around your noon hour?In truth that which you call freedom is the strongest of these chains, though its links glitter in the sun and dazzle the eyes.

And what is it but fragments of your own self you would discard that you may become free? If it is an unjust law you would abolish, that law was written with your own hand upon your own forehead. You cannot erase it by burning your law books nor by washing the foreheads of your judges, though you pour the sea upon them.

And if it is a despot you would dethrone, see first that his throne erected within you is destroyed.

自由

因為，暴君要如何統治自由、尊貴之民？除非他們的自由充滿了暴戾，尊貴滿藏著羞恥。

如果你們想拋捨顧慮，這顧慮乃是你們自找的，絕非來自他人的強迫。

如果你們想驅散憂懼，這憂懼乃居於你們心中，不在於你憂懼之人的手中。

事實上，在你們的生命中運行的所有事物，渴欲和畏懼、厭惡和珍惜、追求和逃避，永遠相偎相倚。

就像光和影，成雙成對地盤旋在你心中。

一旦影子褪淡，不再出現，獨自徘徊的光就會成為另一道光的影子。

而你的自由，一旦失去束縛，就會變成更大自由的束縛。

For how can a tyrant rule the free and the proud, but for a tyranny in their own freedom and a shame in their won pride?

And if it is a care you would cast off, that care has been chosen by you rather than imposed upon you. And if it is a fear you would dispel, the seat of that fear is in your heart and not in the hand of the feared.

Verily all things move within your being in constant half embrace, the desired and the dreaded, the repugnant and the cherished, the pursued and that which you would escape. These things move within you as lights and shadows in pairs that cling.

And when the shadow fades and is no more, the light that lingers becomes a shadow to another light.

And thus your freedom when it loses its fetters becomes itself the fetter of a greater freedom.

15
理性與熱情

女祭司再度開口說，請跟我們談談「理性」和「熱情」。

他於是答道：

你的靈魂經常是個戰場，就是你的理性與判斷、你的熱情與欲望在其中交戰。

多麼希望我能是你靈魂的和平使者，將你本質中的衝突與對立化為協調一致的旋律。

然而，除非你們本身也是和平使者，不，不僅如此，你們還要熱愛自己的一切本質，否則我要如何做到呢？

And the priestess spoke again and said:

"Speak to us of Reason and Passion."

And he answered saying:

Your soul is oftentimes a battlefield, upon which your reason and your judgment wage war against passion and your appetite.

Would that I could be the peacemaker in your soul, that I might turn the discord and the rivalry of your elements into oneness and melody.

But how shall I, unless you yourselves be also the peacemakers, nay, the lovers of all your elements?

　　你的理性和熱情是你的靈魂航海的舵與帆。一旦你的舵或帆破損了，你就得在海上隨波飄流，或者滯留在汪洋大海中。

　　因為，只有理性的支配時，它是局限的力量，而不加約束的熱情是燒毀自我的火苗。

　　因此，讓你的靈魂將理性提昇到熱情的高度，讓靈魂歡欣高歌；並且，讓你的靈魂以理性來引導熱情，你的熱情就能夠日日更新，猶如從灰燼中振翅而起的鳳凰。

　　但願你們在看待自己的判斷和欲望時，把它們當成家裏的貴賓。你們當然不會禮遇其中一人而忽略另一人，因為偏愛一人就會失去兩人的愛與忠實。

　　當你在群山之中，坐在白楊樹蔭下，享受遠方田野和草原的寧靜安詳　讓你的心靜默地說：「神在理性中歇息。」

　　而當暴風雨來臨，強勁的風搖撼著森林，雷聲和閃電在宣示穹蒼的莊嚴　讓你的心敬畏地說：「神在熱情中活動。」

　　你既是神的領域中的一絲氣息，是神的森林中的一片樹葉，就應該在理性中歇息，在熱情中活動。

Your reason and your passion are the rudder and the sails of your seafaring soul. If either your sails or our rudder be broken, you can but toss and drift, or else be held at a standstill in mid-seas.

For reason, ruling alone, is a force confining; and passion, unattended, is a flame that burns to its own destruction.

Therefore let your soul exalt your reason to the height of passion; that it may sing; And let it direct your passion with reason, that your passion may live through its own daily resurrection, and like the phoenix rise above its own ashes.

I would have you consider your judgment and your appetite even as you would two loved guests in your house. Surely you would not honour one guest above the other; for he who is more mindful of one loses the love and the faith of both.

Among the hills, when you sit in the cool shade of the white poplars, sharing the peace and serenity of distant fields and meadows -- then let your heart say in silence, "God rests in reason."

And when the storm comes, and the mighty wind shakes the forest, and thunder and lightning proclaim the majesty of the sky, -- then let your heart say in awe, "God moves in passion."

And since you are a breath In God's sphere, and a leaf in God's forest, you too should rest in reason and move in passion.

16
痛苦

一個婦人開口說，跟我們談談「痛苦」吧。

他答道：

你們的痛苦就是打破圍困你的理解力的外殼。

Ind a woman spoke, saying, "Tell us of Pain."

And he said:

Your pain is the breaking of the shell that encloses your understanding.

痛苦

　　如同果核必須破殼才能暴露在陽光下，你們也必須了解痛苦。

　　倘若你們能對日常生活中的奇蹟保持著驚奇讚嘆的心，那麼痛苦所帶給你的驚喜絕不亞於歡欣；

　　接納你心中的四季，就如同你向來接納拂過你田地上的季節一樣。如此，當憂傷的冬日來臨，你就可以平靜地凝望它。

　　大部分的痛苦都是你們自找的。

　　事實上，這是在你們體內的醫生為了治療你的心病所下的苦藥。因此，信任這位醫生，沉默且平靜地喝下他的藥方。

　　縱使他的手剛硬沉重，卻是由那無形的神溫柔的手所引導，

　　儘管他帶來的杯皿燙傷你的唇，那卻是由神這位陶匠用祂神聖的淚水濕潤泥土燒成的。

Even as the stone of the fruit must break, that its heart may stand in the sun, so must you know pain.

And could you keep your heart in wonder at the daily miracles of your life, your pain would not seem less wondrous than your joy;

And you would accept the seasons of your heart, even as you have always accepted the seasons that pass over your fields.

And you would watch with serenity through the winters of your grief.

Much of your pain is self-chosen.

It is the bitter potion by which the physician within you heals your sick self. Therefore trust the physician, and drink his remedy in silence and tranquillity:

For his hand, though heavy and hard, is guided by the tender hand of the Unseen,

And the cup he brings, though it burn your lips, has been fashioned of the clay which the Potter has moistened with His own sacred tears.

17
自知

一個男人說，和我們談談「自知」吧。

他於是答道：

你們的心在靜默中通曉白晝和黑夜的奧祕。然而，你們的耳卻渴望聽到心的知識。

And a man said, "Speak to us of Self-Knowledge."

And he answered, saying:

Your hearts know in silence the secrets of the days and the nights.

But your ears thirst for the sound of your heart's knowledge.

你意圖將意識的認知轉化為語言的了解。

你要用指尖輕觸夢境赤裸的實體。

你本該這麼做的。

你靈魂中潛隱的井泉必須湧出，一路低吟奔騰入海；

你無可測度的寶藏將在你眼前展現。

但是，別用秤去量測那未知的寶藏；

也不要用長桿或錘繩來尋測你智識的深度。

因為自我乃是不可測度的無垠大海。

不要說「我已尋得真理」，應該說「我已發現一件事實」。

不要說「我已尋得靈魂的道路」，應該說「我遇見走在我路上的靈魂」。

因為靈魂步行在所有的道路上。

靈魂不是走在一條線上，也不像一枝蘆葦般成長。

靈魂會綻放，猶如一朵有無數花瓣的蓮花。

You would know in words that which you have always know in thought.

You would touch with your fingers the naked body of your dreams.

And it is well you should.

The hidden well-spring of your soul must needs rise and run murmuring to the sea; and the treasure of your infinite depths would be revealed to your eyes.

But let there be no scales to weigh your unknown treasure;

And seek not the depths of your knowledge with staff or sounding line.

For self is a sea boundless and measureless.

Say not, "I have found the truth,"
but rather, "I have found a truth."
Say not, "I have found the path of the soul."
Say rather, "I have met the soul walking upon my path."
For the soul walks upon all paths.

The soul walks not upon a line, neither does it grow like a reed.

The soul unfolds itself, like a lotus of countless petals.

18
教育

然後，一個教師說，和我們談談「教育」吧。

他答道：

除了已在你知識的曙光中半醒半睡的事物之外，沒有人能夠教給你什麼。

Then said a teacher, "Speak to us of Teaching."

And he said:

No man can reveal to you aught but that which already lies half asleep in the dawning of our knowledge.

走在神殿的陰影下，處於門徒之間的教師，傳授給人的，與其說是智慧，毋寧說是信實與愛。

他若真有智慧，便不會令你進入他的智識殿堂，反而會引領你跨過自己心靈的門檻。

天文學家儘可和你暢談他對太空的認識，卻無法將他的了解塞進你的腦中。

音樂家縱使能為你唱出充塞於宇宙的音律，卻無法給你捕捉韻律的耳與唱和其聲的音。

鑽研數學科學的人即使可以對你講述計算和測量的方法，卻無法帶領你悠游其中。

因為獨到的洞察力是私人的羽翼，無法外借。

如同在上帝眼中，你們皆是不同的獨立個體，你們對神的認識與對大地的瞭解也必不相同。

The teacher who walks in the shadow of the temple, among his followers, gives not of his wisdom but rather of his faith and his lovingness.

If he is indeed wise he does not bid you enter the house of wisdom, but rather leads you to the threshold of your own mind.

The astronomer may speak to you of his understanding of space, but he cannot give you his understanding.

The musician may sing to you of the rhythm which is in all space, but he cannot give you the ear which arrests the rhythm nor the voice that echoes it.

And he who is versed in the science of numbers can tell of the regions of weight and measure, but he cannot conduct you thither.

For the vision of one man lends not its wings to another man.

And even as each one of you stands alone in God's knowledge, so must each one of you be alone in his knowledge of God and in his understanding of the earth.

19
友誼

一個年輕人接著說，和我們談談「友誼」吧。

他答道：

朋友是你需求的回應。

他是你用愛耕種、用感恩收割的田地。

他也是你的膳食，你的壁爐。

因為，飢餓時你奔向他，需要平靜時你尋找他。

And a youth said, "Speak to us of Friendship."

And he answered, saying:

Your friend is your needs answered.

He is your field which you sow with love and reap with thanksgiving.

And he is your board and your fireside. For you come to him with your hunger, and you seek him for peace.

友誼

　　當你的朋友向你傾訴心聲時，不要害怕在自己心中說「不」，也不要吝於說「是」。

　　而當他沉默不語時，你的心仍可傾聽他的心；因為，在友誼中不需藉助言語，一切思想、一切意念和一切期盼，都在無可言喻的歡愉中孕生而共享。

　　當你和朋友離別時，不要悲傷；因他最得你讚賞的特質在他離去後會更加明顯，一如登山者在平原上遠望時，高山會更加清晰。

　　而且，除了追尋心靈的深耕之外，友誼應當別無所圖。

　　因為，只求展露自己的神秘而無所他求的愛，不能稱之為愛，它只是一張投撒出來的網：捕獲的只是無用之物。

　　把最好的你留給朋友。

　　若他知曉你的低潮，也讓他知道你的高潮。

　　因為，你若只是為了打發時日，要朋友何用？

　　應該邀朋友共享生命才是。

　　因為朋友要帶給你的乃是滿足，不是空虛。

　　就在友誼的滋潤下恣意歡笑，同享喜悅吧。

　　因為你的心將在微瑣事物的露珠中，找到自己的清晨，並且煥然一新。

When your friend speaks his mind you fear not the "nay" in your own mind, nor do you withhold the "ay."

And when he is silent your heart ceases not to listen to his heart; for without words, in friendship, all thoughts, all desires, all expectations are born and shared, with joy that is unacclaimed.

When you part from your friend, you grieve not; for that which you love most in him may be clearer in his absence, as the mountain to the climber is clearer from the plain.

And let there be no purpose in friendship save the deepening of the spirit.

For love that seeks aught but the disclosure of its own mystery is not love but a net cast forth: and only the unprofitable is caught.

And let your best be for your friend.

If he must know the ebb of your tide, let him know its flood also. For what is your friend that you should seek him with hours to kill?

Seek him always with hours to live.

For it is his to fill your need, but not your emptiness.

And in the sweetness of friendship, let there be laughter, and sharing of pleasures.

For in the dew of little things the heart finds its morning and is refreshed.

20
說話

接著一個學者說，談談「說話」吧。

他答道：

說話即是你不再安於思想的表現；

And then a scholar said, "Speak of Talking."

And he answered, saying:

You talk when you cease to be at peace with your thoughts;

當你再也無法安居於心中的孤獨時，你就移居於雙唇，聲音成為消遣和娛樂。

在你大部分的談話中，有半數思想被扼殺。

因為思想乃穹蒼之鳥，或許能在語言的樊籠中展翅，卻無法翱翔其中。

你們之中有人因害怕獨處而依附多話的人。

獨處的靜寂對他們顯露出赤裸的自我，他們因此極欲逃避。

有些人沒有智慧或遠見，卻在談話中揭露出連他們也不明白的真理。

更有些人知曉真理，卻不用語言來表達。

在這種人的胸懷中，靈魂居於有節奏的靜默中。

當你和朋友在路邊或市場相遇時，就讓你的靈魂驅使你的雙唇，指引你的舌頭吧。

讓你心中的聲音進入他的耳中最深處；

因為他的靈魂會保留你心中的真理，正如酒的味道會留在記憶中，

雖然酒的顏色被忘卻，酒樽也不復存在。

And when you can no longer dwell in the solitude of your heart you live in your lips, and sound is a diversion and a pastime.

And in much of your talking, thinking is half murdered.

For thought is a bird of space, that in a cage of words many indeed unfold its wings but cannot fly.

There are those among you who seek the talkative through fear of being alone.

The silence of aloneness reveals to their eyes their naked selves and they would escape.

And there are those who talk, and without knowledge or forethought reveal a truth which they themselves do not understand.

And there are those who have the truth within them, but they tell it not in words. In the bosom of such as these the spirit dwells in rhythmic silence.

When you meet your friend on the roadside or in the market place, let the spirit in you move your lips and direct your tongue.

Let the voice within your voice speak to the ear of his ear;

For his soul will keep the truth of your heart as the taste of the wine is remembered.

When the colour is forgotten and the vessel is no more.

21
時間

一個天文學家問道，大師，關於時間，你的看法又是如何呢？

他答道：

你們想量測無法計數也無從數算的時間。

And an astronomer said, "Master, what of Time?"

And he answered:

You would measure time the measureless and the immeasurable.

你們想依據時辰和季節調整步伐，甚至希望引領心靈的前進。

你們想將時間看成一道溪流，然後端坐堤上，看著它流動。

然而，心中的永恆知道生命的無窮無盡，

明白昨日不過是今日的回憶，而明日乃是今日的夢想。

那在你體內歡唱、沉思的，仍然端居於將星斗撒到空中的太初時刻。

你們之中有誰不認為自己愛的力量是無限的？

誰不會感受到那種愛？愛雖然是無限的，卻僅縈繞在生命的四周，不會在一個又一個愛的念頭中流轉，也不會在一個又一個的行為上游移。

時間不也像愛一樣，無法分割也無速度可言嗎？

但是，在你的想法中，如果必須將時間區分出不同的季節，那就讓每個季節都蘊含所有的季節，

也讓今天用回憶擁抱過去，用渴望擁抱將來。

You would adjust your conduct and even direct the course of your spirit according to hours and seasons.

Of time you would make a stream upon whose bank you would sit and watch its flowing.

Yet the timeless in you is aware of life's timelessness,

And knows that yesterday is but today's memory and tomorrow is today's dream.

And that that which sings and contemplates in you is still dwelling within the bounds of that first moment which scattered the stars into space.

Who among you does not feel that his power to love is boundless?

And yet who does not feel that very love, though boundless, encompassed within the centre of his being, and moving not form love thought to love thought, nor from love deeds to other love deeds?

And is not time even as love is, undivided and placeless?

But if in you thought you must measure time into seasons, let each season encircle all the other seasons,

And let today embrace the past with remembrance and the future with longing.

22
善與惡

城裏有位長者說，我們談談「善」與「惡」吧。

他答道：

我可以談談你們內在的善，卻無法論及你們的惡。

惡不就是被自己的飢渴所折磨的善嗎？

是的，當善飢餓時，它不惜在黑暗的洞穴中覓食，而當善口渴時，它也不惜啜飲死水。

And one of the elders of the city said,

　"Speak to us of Good and Evil."

And he answered:

Of the good in you I can speak, but not of the evil.

For what is evil but good tortured by its own hunger and thirst? Verily when good is hungry it seeks food even in dark caves, and when it thirsts, it drinks even of dead waters.

當你和自己合而為一，你是善良的。

但是當你沒有和自己合而為一，你並不邪惡。

因為，一棟分裂的屋子並不等於賊窩；它不過是一棟分裂的屋子。一艘沒有舵的船，可能只會在危險的群島中漫無目的地漂流，而不至於沉入海底。

當你努力獻出自己時，你是善良的。

然而當你為自己尋求收穫時，你並不邪惡。

因為當你在追求自己的利益時，你只不過是緊攀著大地、吸吮她胸膛的樹根。

當然，果實不可能對樹根說，「要效法我成熟飽滿，而且樂於獻出自己的豐盈。」因為，對果實而言，奉獻是它的需要，正如接受是樹根的需要。

當你在談話時完全清醒，你是善良的，

然而，在你睡著而舌頭仍漫無目的地活動時，你並不邪惡。

即使是結巴的言語，也可能使軟弱的舌頭堅強。

當你以堅定果敢的步伐邁向目標時，你是善良的。

然而，你若跛足走去那兒，也不因此變成邪惡。

因為即使跛足而行，那也不是後退。

但是強壯迅捷的你，可別在瘸子面前跛行，以為那是好意。

You are good when you are one with yourself.

Yet when you are not one with yourself you are not evil.

For a divided house is not a den of thieves; it is only a divided house. And a ship without rudder may wander aimlessly among perilous isles yet sink not to the bottom.

You are good when you strive to give of yourself.

Yet you are not evil when you seek gain for yourself.

For when you strive for gain you are but a root that clings to the earth and sucks at her breast.

Surely the fruit cannot say to the root, "Be like me, ripe and full and ever giving of your abundance." For to the fruit giving is a need, as receiving is a need to the root.

You are good when you are fully awake in your speech,

Yet you are not evil when you sleep while your tongue staggers without purpose.

And even stumbling speech may strengthen a weak tongue.

You are good when you walk to your goal firmly and with bold steps.

Yet you are not evil when you go thither limping.

Even those who limp go not backward.

But you who are strong and swift, see that you do not limp before the lame, deeming it kindness.

善與惡

　　你們的善表現在數算不盡的事物上，但是在你們不善時，也不算是邪惡，你們只是懶散閒蕩罷了。

　　可惜啊！雄鹿並無法教烏龜快跑。

　　你的善在於「大我」有所企盼，而這樣的企盼存在於你們每一個人心中。

　　然而，對部分人來說，這種企盼是奮力衝向海洋的浪潮，攜帶著山丘的秘密和森林的樂章。

　　對其他人來說，企盼是和緩的小溪，迷失在蜿蜒的水道中，流連徘徊，直到抵達海岸。

　　但是，別讓那企盼多的人對企盼少的人說，「為什麼你們這麼慢，又老愛停下來？」

　　因為真正善良的人不會去問赤身露體的人，「你的衣服呢？」也不會去問無家可歸的人，「你的房舍發生了什麼事？」

You are good in countless ways, and you are not evil when you are not good, you are only loitering and sluggard.

Pity that the stags cannot teach swiftness to the turtles.

In your longing for your giant self lies your goodness: and that longing is in all of you.

But in some of you that longing is a torrent rushing with might to the sea, carrying the secrets of the hillsides and the songs of the forest.

And in others it is a flat stream that loses itself in angles and bends and lingers before it reaches the shore.

But let not him who longs much say to him who longs little, "Wherefore are you slow and halting?"

For the truly good ask not the naked, "Where is your garment?" nor the houseless, "What has befallen your house?"

23
祈禱

一個女祭司說，和我們談談「祈禱」吧。

他於是答道：

你們在煩惱與匱乏時祈禱；但願你們也在喜樂滿溢、生活豐饒時祈禱。

因為祈禱不就是把自己擴展到光燦的藍天下嗎？

Then a priestess said, "Speak to us of Prayer."

And he answered, saying:

You pray in your distress and in your need; would that you might pray also in the fullness of your joy and in your days of abundance.

For what is prayer but the expansion of yourself into the living ether?

如果將心中的黑暗傾吐到空中能給你安慰，那麼，將心的黎明傾注於空中也能使你享受歡愉。

如果你的靈魂召喚你祈禱，你卻只能哭泣，它就應該不斷地鼓勵你，直到你展露笑顏。

當你祈禱時，你便飛昇至空中，與那些同時在祈禱的人相會。你只有在祈禱時，才能見到那些人。

因此，就讓你去造訪那無形的神殿，只為了狂喜和醇郁的心靈交流吧。

因為，如果你進神殿無其他目的，只為開口要求，你將一無所獲；

如果你進神殿是為了表示謙卑，神也不會頌揚你，

如果你進神殿是為他人祈求好處，神也不會垂聽。

你只要進入無形的神殿就已足夠。

And if it is for your comfort to pour your darkness into space, it is also for your delight to pour forth the dawning of your heart.

And if you cannot but weep when your soul summons you to prayer, she should spur you again and yet again, though weeping, until you shall come laughing.

When you pray you rise to meet in the air those who are praying at that very hour, and whom save in prayer you may not meet.

Therefore let your visit to that temple invisible be for naught but ecstasy and sweet communion.

For if you should enter the temple for no other purpose than asking you shall not receive.

And if you should enter into it to humble yourself you shall not be lifted;

Or even if you should enter into it to beg for the good of others you shall not be heard.

It is enough that you enter the temple invisible.

我無法教你們怎麼說祈禱詞。

除非上帝藉由你們的唇說話，否則祂不會傾聽你們的言語。

我也無法教你們大海、森林和高山的祈禱詞。

然而，你們這些出生於大海、森林及高山諸地的人，可以在心中找到它們的祈禱詞，

如果你們在沉靜的夜裏傾聽，你們必會聽見它們默默地說：「我們的神啊，你是我們長著羽翼的自我，你的意願就是我們心中的意願。

你的需欲就是我們心中的需欲。

你在我們心中的激勵使得黑夜變成白晝。

我們無法向你要求什麼，因為在我們開口之前，你早已知曉我們的需要。

你就是我們的需要；在你不斷付出自己時，你將一切都賜給了我們。」

I can not teach you how to pray in words.

God listens not to your words save when He Himself utters them through your lips.

And I cannot teach you the prayer of the seas and the forests and the mountains.

But you who are born of the mountains and the forests and the seas can find their prayer in your heart,

And if you but listen in the stillness of the night you shall hear them saying in silence,

"Our God, who art our winged self, it is thy will in us that willeth.It is thy desire in us that desireth.

It is thy urge in us that would turn our nights, which are thine, into days which are thine also.

We cannot ask thee for aught, for thou knowest our needs before they are born in us:

Thou art our need; and in giving us more of thyself thou givest us all."

24
歡樂

然後，一個每年進城一次的隱士說，

和我們談談「歡樂」吧。

他於是答道：

歡樂是一首自由之歌，

但並不是自由。

Then a hermit, who visited the city once a year, came forth
and said, "Speak to us of Pleasure."

And he answered, saying:

Pleasure is a freedom song,

But it is not freedom.

它是你的願望綻開的花朵，
卻不是願望結出的果實。
它是深谷對高峰的呼喊，
但是它既不是深谷也不是高山。
它是籠中鳥展翅，
但不是無垠的空間。
哎，說真的，歡樂是一首自由之歌。
我希望你們全心全意地唱出這首歌謠，但不希望你們在歡唱中迷失了本心。

在你們之中，有些年輕人竭力尋求歡樂，以為它就是一切，他們也因此受到批評與斥責。
我卻不會批評或斥責他們。我會讓他們去追尋。
因為他們將會尋得歡樂，但尋獲的並不只是歡樂；
歡樂有七個姊妹，其中最差的也比歡樂還要嬌美。
難道你們不曾聽說，有人在挖掘樹根時找到了寶藏？

It is the blossoming of your desires,

But it is not their fruit.

It is a depth calling unto a height,

But it is not the deep nor the high.

It is the caged taking wing,

But it is not space encompassed.

Ay, in very truth, pleasure is a freedom-song.

And I fain would have you sing it with fullness of heart; yet I would not have you lose your hearts in the singing.

Some of your youth seek pleasure as if it were all, and they are judged and rebuked.

I would not judge nor rebuke them. I would have them seek.

For they shall find pleasure, but not her alone:

Seven are her sisters, and the least of them is more beautiful than pleasure. Have you not heard of the man who was digging in the earth for roots and found a treasure?

在你們之中有些老人，以懊悔的心情追憶往昔的歡樂，彷彿那是醉酒時犯下的過錯。

然而懊悔只是使心靈蒙上陰影，而不是懲罰。

應該以感恩的心追懷昔日歡樂，就像豐收時回憶夏季。

但是懊悔若能給他們安慰，就讓他們獲得安慰吧。

在你們之中還有些人，既不是愛追尋的年輕人，也不是愛回憶的老年人；

在害怕追尋和恐懼回憶的情況下，他們躲開所有歡樂，以免忽視心靈或觸怒心靈。

然而，即使是這樣，他們仍會感到歡樂。

雖是以顫抖的雙手挖掘樹根，他們也獲得寶藏了。

但是，告訴我，誰能觸怒心靈呢？

夜鶯會觸怒夜的寂靜嗎？螢火蟲會觸怒滿天星斗嗎？

你們的火焰與煙灰會成為風的負擔嗎？

你認為心靈是一座平靜的池水，可以被你用一支長竿攪亂嗎？

And some of your elders remember pleasures with regret like wrongs committed in drunkenness. But regret is the beclouding of the mind and not its chastisement.

They should remember their pleasures with gratitude, as they would the harvest of a summer.

Yet if it comforts them to regret, let them be comforted.

And there are among you those who are neither young to seek nor old to remember;

And in their fear of seeking and remembering they shun all pleasures, lest they neglect the spirit or offend against it.

But even in their foregoing is their pleasure.

And thus they too find a treasure though they dig for roots with quivering hands.

But tell me, who is he that can offend the spirit?

Shall the nightingale offend the stillness of the night, or the firefly the stars?

And shall your flame or your smoke burden the wind?

Think you the spirit is a still pool which you can trouble with a staff?

通常，在你拒絕追尋歡樂時，你只不過是把欲望積存在內心深處。

誰知道，那些在今天被暫忘的事，不會等著在明天出現？

甚至你的肉體也知道它天賦的權利和正當的需求，而不被欺瞞。你的肉體乃是你靈魂的豎琴。

它要奏出優美的旋律或混亂的噪音，都取決於你自己。

此刻，你心生疑問，「我們要如何分辨歡樂中的好和不好呢？」走到你的田野和花園，你就會明白，蜜蜂的歡樂在於採集花蜜。

而獻出花蜜給蜜蜂也是花朵的歡樂。

因為，對蜜蜂而言，花朵是生命的泉源，

對花朵而言，蜜蜂則是愛的信使，

對蜜蜂和花朵雙方而言，歡樂的收受是一種需要，也是極樂。

奧菲里斯城的人啊，享受你們的歡樂吧，就如同蜜蜂和花朵沉醉在它們的歡樂之中。

Oftentimes in denying yourself pleasure you do but store the desire in the recesses of your being.

Who knows but that which seems omitted today, waits for tomorrow?

Even your body knows its heritage and its rightful need and will not be deceived. And your body is the harp of your soul,

And it is yours to bring forth sweet music from it or confused sounds.

And now you ask in your heart, "How shall we distinguish that which is good in pleasure from that which is not good?"

Go to your fields and your gardens, and you shall learn that it is the pleasure of the bee to gather honey of the flower,

But it is also the pleasure of the flower to yield its honey to the bee.

For to the bee a flower is a fountain of life,

And to the flower a bee is a messenger of love,

And to both, bee and flower, the giving and the receiving of pleasure is a need and an ecstasy.

People of Orphalese, be in your pleasures like the flowers and the bees.

25
美

接著，一個詩人說，和我們談談「美」吧。

他答道：

你們該往何處追尋美呢？除非她是你們的道路、你們的嚮導，否則你們要如何尋見她呢？

除非她是你們言詞的編織者，否則你們要如何談論她呢？

And a poet said, "Speak to us of Beauty."

And he answered:

Where shall you seek beauty, and how shall you find her unless she herself be your way and your guide?

And how shall you speak of her except she be the weaver of your speech?

美

哀愁與受傷的人說，「美是仁慈、溫柔的。她走在我們之中，就像一個年輕的母親，對自己的榮光半帶羞澀。」

熱情的人則說，「不，美是強大可畏的東西。

就像暴風雨一樣，撼動了我們腳下的地和頭上的天。」

疲倦、困乏的人說，「美是輕柔的呢喃。她在我們的心靈說話。她的聲音屈服於我們的沉默，就像一抹微光，因害怕陰影而顫抖。」

坐立不安的人卻說，「我們曾聽見她在群山間呼喊，她的喊叫帶來了馬蹄聲、拍翅聲和獅群的吼聲。」

入夜時，城中的守夜者說，「美將隨著黎明從東方升起。」

正午時，辛勞工作的人和徒步旅行的人說，「我們曾在晚霞的窗口看到她斜倚在大地上。」

在冬季，困在雪中的人說，「她將隨著春天來臨，在山丘間跳躍。」

在夏季的酷熱中，收割的人說，「我們看見她和秋季的葉片共舞，還看到她的髮梢沾著雪花。」

The aggrieved and the injured say, "Beauty is kind and gentle.Like a young mother half-shy of her own glory she walks among us."

And the passionate say, "Nay, beauty is a thing of might and dread.Like the tempest she shakes the earth beneath us and the sky above us."

The tired and the weary say, "Beauty is of soft whisperings. She speaks in our spirit. Her voice yields to our silences like a faint light that quivers in fear of the shadow."

But the restless say, "We have heard her shouting among the mountains,

And with her cries came the sound of hoofs, and the beating of wings and the roaring of lions."

At night the watchmen of the city say, "Beauty shall rise with the dawn from the east."

And at noontide the toilers and the wayfarers say, "We have seen her leaning over the earth from the windows of the sunset."

In winter say the snow-bound, "She shall come with the spring leaping upon the hills."

And in the summer heat the reapers say, "We have seen her dancing with the autumn leaves, and we saw a drift of snow in her hair."

美

這些都是你們對美的敘述，

然而，事實上，你們敘述的不是美，而是你們未獲得滿足的需求，

但是，美不是需求，而是狂喜。

它不是乾渴的嘴，也不是一隻往前伸出的空手，

而是熾熱的心和充滿魅力的靈魂。

它不是你們看得見的影像，也不是你們聽得見的歌謠，

而是你們雖閉起雙眼仍能見到的影像，掩住耳朵仍能聽聞的歌謠。

它不是粗皺樹皮下的汁液，也不是連接指爪的翅翼，

而是一座永遠開花的花園，一群恆常飛翔的天使。

奧菲里斯城的人哪，美就是卸下面紗，露出神聖容顏的生命。

然而，你們就是生命，你們就是面紗。

美是永恆，凝視著鏡中的自己。

而你們就是永恆，你們就是鏡子。

All these things have you said of beauty,

Yet in truth you spoke not of her but of needs unsatisfied,

And beauty is not a need but an ecstasy.

It is not a mouth thirsting nor an empty hand stretched forth,

But rather a heart enflamed and a soul enchanted.

It is not the image you would see nor the song you would hear,

But rather an image you see though you close your eyes and a song you hear though you shut your ears.

It is not the sap within the furrowed bark, nor a wing attached to a claw,

But rather a garden for ever in bloom and a flock of angels for ever in flight.

People of Orphalese, beauty is life when life unveils her holy face.

But you are life and you are the veil. Beauty is eternity gazing at itself in a mirror.

But you are eternity and you are the mirror.

26
宗教

一位老祭司說，和我們談談「宗教」吧。

他答道：

我今天說了些別的嗎？

宗教不就是所有的行為和思想，

以及那既非行為也非思想，而是當雙手挫鑿石頭或操作織布機時，仍在靈魂中閃現的神奇和驚喜嗎？

誰能將自己的信仰和行為分開，或者將信念從工作中分出呢？

And an old priest said, "Speak to us of Religion."

And he said:

Have I spoken this day of aught else?

Is not religion all deeds and all reflection,

And that which is neither deed nor reflection, but a wonder and a surprise ever springing in the soul, even while the hands hew the stone or tend the loom?

Who can separate his faith from his actions, or his belief from his occupations?

誰能將自己的時間在眼前攤開,然後說,「這是給神的,這是給我的;這些給我的靈魂,剩下的就給我的肉體?」

你所擁有的全部時光,都是宇宙裏鼓動的羽翼,從自我飛向自我。把道德當成華服穿在身上的人,還不如一絲不掛。風和太陽並不會在他的皮膚上撕剝出洞來。

而那以倫理來界定自己行為的人,便是將他的鳴禽關在籠中。最自由的歌聲絕無法出自鐵絲和柵欄。

有人把敬拜當成一扇可以開也可以關的窗戶,這樣的人還不曾探訪過自己的靈魂之屋,那裏的窗子是從黎明敞開到黎明的。

你的日常生活就是你的神殿,你的宗教。

不論何時,只要你進去參拜,都應當帶著你的一切。

帶著犁和鍛鐵爐,還有木槌和琴,以及那些你為了需要和歡樂而製造的器具。因為,在你的幻想中,你無法高於你的成就,也不會低於你的挫敗。

你要帶所有人前去:

因為在禮拜時,你無法飛得比他們的希望高,也不會謙卑得比他們的失望低。

如果你想認識神,就不要做一個解謎者。

看看四周,你將看見祂正和你的孩子一同嬉戲。

然後看看天空;你將看到祂在雲端行走,在閃電中伸展臂膀,在雨水中降臨。

你將看到祂在花中微笑,然後在樹林間揮手升天。

Who can spread his hours before him, saying, "This for God and this for myself; This for my soul, and this other for my body?" All your hours are wings that beat through space from self to self.

He who wears his morality but as his best garment were better naked. The wind and the sun will tear no holes in his skin. And he who defines his conduct by ethics imprisons his song-bird in a cage.

The freest song comes not through bars and wires.

And he to whom worshipping is a window, to open but also to shut, has not yet visited the house of his soul whose windows are from dawn to dawn.

Your daily life is your temple and your religion.

Whenever you enter into it take with you your all.

Take the plough and the forge and the mallet and the lute,

The things you have fashioned in necessity or for delight.

For in revery you cannot rise above your achievements nor fall lower than your failures.

And take with you all men:

For in adoration you cannot fly higher than their hopes nor humble yourself lower than their despair.

And if you would know God be not therefore a solver of riddles. Rather look about you and you shall see Him playing with your children. And look into space; you shall see Him walking in the cloud, outstretching His arms in the lightning and descending in rain. You shall see Him smiling in flowers, then rising and waving His hands in trees.

27
死亡

然後，艾蜜特拉說，現在我們要問一問「死亡」。

他答道：

你們想知曉死亡的奧秘，

除非你們在生命的中心尋覓，否則如何能找到答案？

Than Almitra spoke, saying,

  "We would ask now of Death."

And he said:

You would know the secret of death.

But how shall you find it unless you seek it in the heart of life?

死亡

雙眼只能識得夜間景物的貓頭鷹，在白晝是眼盲的，因此無法揭開光的奧秘。

如果你真想掌握死亡的魂魄，那麼就對生命之體敞開心門吧。因為生與死乃是一體，猶如溪流和大海本屬同源。

在希望與欲念的深處，存在著你對來世沉默的理解；
猶如冰雪覆蓋著種子的夢想，你的心也憧憬著春天。
信賴你的憧憬吧，因為其中潛藏著通往永恆的大門。
你對死亡的恐懼，不過是牧羊人站在國王面前的顫抖，因為國王即將用手輕觸他以表揚他。
外表顫懼的牧羊人，內心豈不因國王親授榮譽而充滿喜樂？
然而，他不是更在意自己的顫懼嗎？
死亡不就是赤裸地佇立於風中，在太陽下融化嗎？
停止呼吸又是什麼？不就是使氣息從永無休止的潮汐中解放，使它升騰、擴展，無阻礙地尋求神嗎？

唯有在啜飲了靜默之河的水，你才能真正歌唱。
唯有在抵達山巔之時，你才能開始攀爬。
唯有在大地要收回你的肢體時，你才能真正地跳舞。

On Death

The owl whose night-bound eyes are blind unto the day cannot unveil the mystery of light.

If you would indeed behold the spirit of death, open your heart wide unto the body of life.For life and death are one, even as the river and the sea are one.

In the depth of your hopes and desires lies your silent knowledge of the beyond; And like seeds dreaming beneath the snow your heart dreams of spring.

Trust the dreams, for in them is hidden the gate to eternity.

Your fear of death is but the trembling of the shepherd when he stands before the king whose hand is to be laid upon him in honour. Is the sheered not joyful beneath his trembling, that he shall wear the mark of the king?

Yet is he not more mindful of his trembling?

For what is it to die but to stand naked in the wind and to melt into the sun?

And what is to cease breathing, but to free the breath from its restless tides, that it may rise and expand and seek God unencumbered?

Only when you drink form the river of silence shall you indeed sing. And when you have reached the mountain top, then you shall begin to climb. And when the earth shall claim your limbs, then shall you truly dance.

28
離別

現在已是黃昏時候。

女預言家艾蜜特拉說，但願此時、此地和你曾開口的心靈都蒙祝福。

他回答說，我是開口說話的人嗎？

我不也是個聽眾嗎？

And now it was evening.

And Almitra the seeress said,

"Blessed be this day and this place and your spirit that has spoken."

And he answered, Was it I who spoke?

Was I not also a listener?

　　然後，他走下神的台階，全城的人都跟著他。他跨上他的船，站在甲板上。

　　他再次面對群眾，揚聲說道：

　　奧菲里斯城的人哪，風要我離開你們了。

　　雖然我不像風那般性急，我仍必須離去。

　　我們這樣的流浪者，總是在尋覓更孤寂的道路，從沒有在過完一天的地方開始另一天，也不會在落日離開我們的地方迎接日出。即使大地入睡了，我們仍在旅行。

　　我們是頑強的植物種子，在我們心靈飽滿時，便將自己獻上，隨風遠颺。

　　儘管我們相聚的時日不多，我所說的話更為簡短。

　　然而，一旦我的話在你們耳中模糊，我的愛於你們記憶中隱沒時，我會再回來。

　　帶著更豐富的心和更依順心靈的唇再度開口。

　　是的，我將乘著浪潮歸來，即使死亡掩蔽我，沉寂緊擁住我，我也會再次尋求你們的了解。

　　而且這樣的尋求絕不落空。

　　倘若我曾傳述真理，那麼，這真理必會以更明晰的聲音、更接近你們思想的文字來顯現。

Then he descended the steps of the Temple and all the people followed him. And he reached his ship and stood upon the deck.

And facing the people again, he raised his voice and said:

People of Orphalese, the wind bids me leave you.

Less hasty am I than the wind, yet I must go.

We wanderers, ever seeking the lonelier way, begin no day where we have ended another day; and no sunrise finds us where sunset left us.Even while the earth sleeps we travel.

We are the seeds of the tenacious plant, and it is in our ripeness and our fullness of heart that we are given to the wind and are scattered.

Brief were my days among you, and briefer still the words I have spoken.

But should my voice fade in your ears, and my love vanish in your memory, then I will come again, and with a richer heart and lips more yielding to the spirit will I speak.

Yea, I shall return with the tide,

And though death may hide me, and the greater silence enfold me, yet again will I seek your understanding.

And not in vain will I seek.

If aught I have said is truth, that truth shall reveal itself in a clearer voice, and in words more kin to your thoughts.

奧菲里斯城的人哪，我將御風而去，卻不會陷於虛空；

倘使今日無法滿足你們的要求和我的愛，就讓它成為允諾直到另一天來到。

人的需求會變，心中的愛卻不會，想要用愛來滿足需求的欲望也是一樣。

因此，你們要明白，我將自更深的靜默中歸來。

黎明驅散晨霧，留下朝露於田間，但霧靄將升騰凝聚成雲，然後化成雨水降臨。

我彷似晨霧。

在夜的靜寂中，我行過你們的街道，精神探進你們的屋宅，

你們的心跳聲在我的心中，你們的呼吸吹在我臉上，我認得你們每一個人。是啊，我知道你們的歡樂和痛苦，而當你們沉睡時，你們的夢就是我的夢。

我在你們中間猶如群山環繞的湖泊。

我映照出你們的山顛、陡坡，甚至如羊群般掠過你們心中的思緒和欲望。

孩童的歡笑是小溪，青年的盼望是河流，全都匯聚到我的靜默中。

他們來到我的內心深處時，依然歡唱不歇。

然而，比歡笑更甜美，比盼望更強烈的東西也流進我心中。

那就是你們廣闊無垠的心；

I go with the wind, people of Orphalese, but not down into emptiness;

And if this day is not a fulfillment of your needs and my love, then let it be a promise till another day.

Man's needs change, but not his love, nor his desire that his love should satisfy his needs.

Know therefore, that from the greater silence I shall return.

The mist that drifts away at dawn, leaving but dew in the fields, shall rise and gather into a cloud and then fall down in rain.

And not unlike the mist have I been.

In the stillness of the night I have walked in your streets, and my spirit has entered your houses,

And your heart-beats were in my heart, and your breath was upon my face, and I knew you all. Ay, I knew your joy and your pain, and in your sleep your dreams were my dreams.

And oftentimes I was among you a lake among the mountains.

I mirrored the summits in you and the bending slopes, and even the passing flocks of your thoughts and your desires.

And to my silence came the laughter of your children in streams, and the longing of your youths in rivers.

And when they reached my depth the streams and the rivers ceased not yet to sing.

But sweeter still than laughter and greater than longing came to me. It was boundless in you;

它是個大巨人，你們都只是他裏面的細胞和筋腱；

在他的唱頌下，你們的歌唱不過是無聲的悸動。

唯有在巨人裏面，你們才會巨大，

唯有在注視他時，我才能瞧見你們，並且愛你們。

因為，在那巨大的領域內，有什麼距離是愛無法跨越的呢？

什麼樣的景像、什麼樣的盼望和什麼樣的推量能高飛過他呢？

你們心中的巨人就像一棵滿覆蘋果花的高大橡樹。

他的大能使你們與大地連結，他的香氣使你們升到空中，他的堅毅使你們不朽。

有人告訴過你們，就像在一條鎖鍊中，你們是其中最弱的一環。這話只說對了一半，因為，你們也是鎖鍊中最強固的一環。

以你們最微小的行為來審度你們，就如同以最微弱的泡沫來裁定海洋的力量一樣。

以你們的失敗來評斷你們，就如同以易變無常來責備四季一樣。

The vast man in whom you are all but cells and sinews;

He in whose chant all your singing is but a soundless throbbing.

It is in the vast man that you are vast,

And in beholding him that I beheld you and loved you.

For what distances can love reach that are not in that vast sphere? What visions, what expectations and what presumptions can outsoar that flight?

Like a giant oak tree covered with apple blossoms is the vast man in you.

His mind binds you to the earth, his fragrance lifts you into space, and in his durability you are deathless.

You have been told that, even like a chain, you are as weak as your weakest link. This is but half the truth. You are also as strong as your strongest link.

To measure you by your smallest deed is to reckon the power of ocean by the frailty of its foam.

To judge you by your failures is to cast blame upon the seasons for their inconsistency.

是的，你們彷如大海，

即使擱淺的船隻在你們岸邊等待潮起，你們仍如同大海，無法催促海水漲潮。

你們也像四季，雖然在嚴冬時拒絕了春天，然而，在你們裏面暫歇的春天，卻在沉寂中微笑，不曾慍怒。

不要誤解我這些話而相互傳告，「他很誇讚我們。他只看到我們好的一面。」

我只是把你們本身知道的事說給你們聽。

什麼是語言知識？不過是非語言知識的影子。

你們的思想和我的話都是從封緘的記憶之海湧出的浪潮，而那記憶之海保存了我們往昔的記錄，也保存了遠古歲月的記錄，那時大地尚未認識我們，也不知道自己，更保存了夜晚的記錄，那時大地因混沌迷惑而情緒激昂。

智者曾來到這裏，把他們的智慧傳授給你們。我來到這裏卻是要接受你們的智慧：

看哪，我已找到比智慧更重大的東西。

那是在你們體內愈燃愈旺的心靈烈焰，

但是，你們卻不留意它的擴展，只為凋萎逝去的時日哀嘆。

只有追求肉體生命的人才會懼怕墳墓。這裏沒有墳墓。

這些山林和平原是搖籃，也是踏腳石。

你們越過祖先安息的草原時，仔細看看四周，就會看見你們自己正在和子女手牽手舞蹈。

真的，你們常常在不知不覺中作樂。

Ay, you are like an ocean,

And though heavy-grounded ships await the tide upon your shores, yet, even like an ocean, you cannot hasten your tides.

And like the seasons you are also, and though in your winter you deny your spring, yet spring, reposing within you, smiles in her drowsiness and is not offended.

Think not I say these things in order that you may say the one to the other, "He praised us well. He saw but the good in us."

I only speak to you in words of that which you yourselves know in thought. And what is word knowledge but a shadow of wordless knowledge? Your thoughts and my words are waves from a sealed memory that keeps records of our yesterdays,

And of the ancient days when the earth knew not us nor herself, and of nights when earth was up wrought with confusion, wise men have come to you to give you of their wisdom. I came to take of your wisdom:

And behold I have found that which is greater than wisdom.

It is a flame spirit in you ever gathering more of itself, while you, heedless of its expansion, bewail the withering of your days.

It is life in quest of life in bodies that fear the grave.

There are no graves here.

These mountains and plains are a cradle and a stepping-stone.

Whenever you pass by the field where you have laid your ancestors look well thereupon, and you shall see yourselves and your children dancing hand in hand.

Verily you often make merry without knowing.

其他人也曾來過,依你們的忠信許下黃金般的承諾,而你們也報以財富、權力和榮耀。

我未給予你們任何承諾,你們回報我卻更為豐厚。

你們給予我比生命更深的渴求。

當然,給人的最大贈禮,莫過於將他一切目標變為灼熱的唇,以及將他全部的生命變成湧泉。

我的榮耀和報酬就在這裏——

無論何時,只要我到湧泉邊喝水,我就會發現這活水本身也是渴的;

我掬飲它時,它也啜飲著我。

你們有些人認為,我因驕傲和過於羞怯而拒收禮物。

我的確是驕傲得無法接受俸祿,但並非不接受禮物。

雖然你們邀我圍坐桌邊時,我在山林間吃食野果,

你們樂於邀我同住時,我在神殿的廊下安眠,

然而,豈不是因著你們對我的關懷,才使我的食物香甜、睡眠有夢?

我要為此特別地祝福你們:

你們付出良多,自己卻不知道。

確實,當仁慈關愛凝視著鏡中的自己,就會變成石頭,

而善行以溫柔美名自稱時,就會成為咒詛的根源。

Others have come to you to whom for golden promises made unto your faith you have given but riches and power and glory.

Less than a promise have I given, and yet more generous have you been to me.

You have given me deeper thirsting after life.

Surely there is no greater gift to a man than that which turns all his aims into parching lips and all life into a fountain.

And in this lies my honour and my reward, --

That whenever I come to the fountain to drink I find the living water itself thirsty; And it drinks me while I drink it.

Some of you have deemed me proud and over-shy to receive gifts. To proud indeed am I to receive wages, but not gifts.

And though I have eaten berries among the hill when you would have had me sit at your board,

And slept in the portico of the temple where you would gladly have sheltered me,

Yet was it not your loving mindfulness of my days and my nights that made food sweet to my mouth and girdled my sleep with visions?

For this I bless you most:

You give much and know not that you give at all.

Verily the kindness that gazes upon itself in a mirror turns to stone, And a good deed that calls itself by tender names becomes the parent to a curse.

　　你們有些人說我孤高，在自己的孤寂中沉醉，你們還說，「他和林中的樹木談笑，卻不與人來往。他獨坐於山巔，俯視我們的城市。」

　　我確曾登高，也確曾在遠方行走。

　　但我若不從高處眺望或從遠處觀看，我如何見得到你們？

　　一個人若不曾置身遠處，豈能真得親近呢？

　　你們當中還有些人默默呼喚我，對我說：

　　「陌生人，陌生人，高不可及之處的愛好者，你為何要居於鷹類築巢的山巔呢？你為何要尋覓得不著的事物呢？你的網是要捕攫什麼樣的狂風疾雨？

　　你欲從中射獵什麼樣的空幻靈鳥呢？加入我們，和我們在一起吧。下來吧，用我們的麵包止飢，用我們的酒解渴。」

　　在靈魂的孤寂處，他們說了這些話；然而，若他們的孤寂更深，他們將會發覺，我尋覓的不過是你們歡樂與痛苦的奧秘，我捕獵的只是你們遊走天空的大我。

　　不過，狩獵者同時也是獵物；

　　因為由我弓中射出的許多利箭，乃以我的胸膛為目標。

　　而飛翔的同時也是爬行的；

　　因為，一旦我在太陽下展翅，雙翼在地上的投影卻是烏龜。

　　我既是相信者也是懷疑者；

　　因為我常用手指撫觸我的傷口，希望能對你們更有信心，更了解你們。

And some of you have called me aloof, and drunk with my own aloneness, and you have said, "He holds council with the trees of the forest, but not with men. he sits alone on hill-tops and looks down upon our city."

True it is that I have climbed the hills and walked in remote places.

How could I have seen you save from a great height or a great distance? How can one be indeed near unless he be far?

And others among you called unto me, not in words, and they said, Stranger, stranger, lover of unreachable heights, why dwell you among the summits where eagles build their nests? why seek you the unattainable? what storms would you trap in your net,

And what vaporous birds do you hunt in the sky? Come and be one of us. Descend and appease your hunger with our bread and quench your thirst with our wine.

In the solitude of their souls they said these things;

But were their solitude deeper they would have known that I sought but the secret of your joy and your pain, and I hunted only your larger selves that walk the sky.

But the hunter was also the hunted: For many of my arrows left my bow only to seek my own breast.

And the flier was also the creeper; For when my wings were spread in the sun their shadow upon the earth was a turtle.

And I the believer was also the doubter; For often have I put my finger in my own wound that I might have the greater belief in you and the greater knowledge of you.

離別

　　憑著這樣的信心和了解，我說，你們並不局限於自己的身體，也不受家園或田地的束縛。

　　你住在山巒之上，隨風飛翔。

　　你們不是為取暖而爬向陽光，也不是為安全而於黑暗中鑿洞，你是自由的，你是擁抱大地、在大氣中游移的魂魄。

　　如果這些話意思模糊，就不要去澄清。

　　模糊和混沌本來就是萬物的開端，而非結束，

　　而且我希望你們記得我是開端。

　　生活以及一切生命都孕生於迷霧中，而非水晶。

　　何況，又有誰知道水晶不是消退的迷霧？

　　我希望你們在憶起我時，能記著這些事：

　　你們體內看似最軟弱最惶惑的部分，卻是最剛強最堅毅的部分。支撐你的骨骼，強固其架構的不就是你的呼吸嗎？

　　構築你們的城市，形成上面所有一切的，不就是你們那不復記憶的夢境嗎？

　　你若看得見呼吸的起伏，就看不見其他事物，

　　你若聽得見夢境的低語，就無法聽見其他聲音。

And it is with this belief and this knowledge that I say,

You are not enclosed within your bodies, nor confined to houses or fields.

That which is you dwells above the mountain and roves with the wind.

It is not a thing that crawls into the sun for warmth or digs holes into darkness for safety, but a thing free, a spirit that envelops the earth and moves in the ether.

If this be vague words, then seek not to clear them.

Vague and nebulous is the beginning of all things, but not their end, and I fain would have you remember me as a beginning.

Life, and all that lives, is conceived in the mist and not in the crystal. And who knows but a crystal is mist in decay?

This would I have you remember in remembering me:

That which seems most feeble and bewildered in you is the strongest and most determined. Is it not your breath that has erected and hardened the structure of your bones?

And is it not a dream which none of you remember having dreamt that building your city and fashioned all there is in it?

Could you but see the tides of that breath you would cease to see all else, and if you could hear the whispering of the dream you would hear no other sound.

然而，你看不見、聽不到卻是好事。

那遮蔽你雙眼的輕紗，將要被編織它的手揭開，

那阻塞你雙耳的泥塊，將要被塑造它的手指捏成碎屑。

於是你就可看見，你即可聽見。

然而，不要悲痛曾經眼盲，也不要懊悔曾經耳聾。

因為，在那一天，你們將知曉萬物在冥冥中的目的，

你將會祝福黑暗，猶如你祝福光明。

說完這些話，他舉目四望，看見他船上的舵手立於舵前，時而凝視漲滿的風帆，時而遠眺天際。

他於是說道：

我的船長很有耐心，極具耐心。

大風揚起，帆在飄盪，

就連方向舵也在請我指引，

我的船長卻靜候我沉默下來。

我的水手們雖曾聽聞大海雄壯的歌聲，

卻依舊耐心地聽我說話。

現在，他們不用再等了。

我已準備就緒。

川流已抵大海，偉大的母親再一次將她的愛子擁入懷中。

But you do not see, nor do you hear, and it is well.

The veil that clouds your eyes shall be lifted by the hands that wove it, and the clay that fills your ears shall be pierced by those fingers that kneaded it.

And you shall see, and you shall hear.

Yet you shall not deplore having known blindness, nor regret having been deaf.

For in that day you shall know the hidden purposes in all things, and you shall bless darkness as you would bless light.

After saying these things he looked about him, and he saw the pilot of his ship standing by the helm and gazing now at the full sails and now at the distance.

And he said:

Patient, over-patient, is the captain of my ship.

The wind blows, and restless are the sails;

Even the rudder begs direction; Yet quietly my captain awaits my silence.

And these my mariners, who have heard the choir of the greater sea, they too have heard me patiently.

Now they shall wait no longer.

I am ready.

The stream has reached the sea, and once more the great mother holds her son against her breast.

再見了，奧菲里斯城的人民。

今日已近尾聲。它已在我們眼前垂上簾幕，正如睡蓮對明日閤起自己的花瓣。

我們在此所得的一切都將留存，如果這一切還不夠，我們便得再次聚集，向施予者伸手要求。

別忘了，我必再度歸來。

再過一會兒，我的期盼就要聚集塵土和泡沫，成為另一具身軀。

再過一會兒，在風上暫歇之後，另一個女人將生下我。

眾人啊，還有我與你們共度的青春，再見了。

我們夢中的相逢彷如昨日。

在我孤獨時，你們對我高歌；在你們的盼望下，我於天空築了高樓。

而今我們的睡眠已經逃離，好夢已盡，黎明不再。

正午已至，半睡已成全醒，我們必須分別。

若我們將於記憶的薄暮時分重逢，我們將再度談笑，你們會再為我唱一首更深沈的歌。若我們的雙手能在另一個夢中交握，我們將於空中另起高樓。

說著，他便向水手們作了個手勢，立即起錨，船離開停泊處，航向東方。

The Farewell

Fare you well, people of Orphalese.

This day has ended.It is closing upon us even as the water-lily upon its own tomorrow.

What was given us here we shall keep, and if it suffices not, then again must we come together and together stretch our hands unto the giver.

Forget not that I shall come back to you.

A little while, and my longing shall gather dust and foam for another body. A little while, a moment of rest upon the wind, and another woman shall bear me.

Farewell to you and the youth I have spent with you.

It was but yesterday we met in a dream.

You have sung to me in my aloneness, and I of your longings have built a tower in the sky.

But now our sleep has fled and our dream is over, and it is no longer dawn.

The noontide is upon us and our half waking has turned to fuller day, and we must part.

If in the twilight of memory we should meet once more, we shall speak again together and you shall sing to me a deeper song. And if our hands should meet in another dream, we shall build another tower in the sky.

So saying he made a signal to the seamen, and straightaway they weighed anchor and cast the ship loose from its moorings, and they moved eastward.

　　眾人的哭聲彷彿發自同一顆心，傳入薄暮，奔向大海，如同巨大的號角聲。

　　只有艾蜜特拉默然凝視著船，直至它消失在霧中。

　　當人們盡皆散去，她依然獨自佇立於海堤上，在心中默想他的話語：

　　「再過一會兒，在風上暫歇之後，另一個女人將生下我。」

And a cry came from the people as from a single heart, and it rose the dusk and was carried out over the sea like a great trumpeting.

Only Almitra was silent, gazing after the ship until it had vanished into the mist.

And when all the people were dispersed she still stood alone upon the sea-wall, remembering in her heart his saying,

"A little while, a moment of rest upon the wind, and another woman shall bear me."

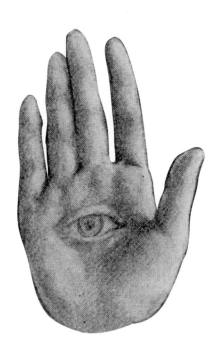

國家圖書館出版品預行編目 (CIP) 資料

先知（中英雙語典藏版）/ 卡里·紀伯倫（Kahlil Gibran）著；
楊宛靜繪；曾惠昭譯 . -- 二版 . -- 臺中市：晨星出版有限公司，
2024.04
　　面； 公分 . --（愛藏本：124）
中英雙語典藏版
譯自：The Prophet

ISBN 978-626-320-809-4（精裝）

865.751　　　　　　　　　　　　　　　　113003497

愛藏本：124
先知（中英雙語典藏版）
The Prophet

作　　者｜卡里·紀伯倫（Kahlil Gibran）
繪　　者｜楊宛靜
譯　　者｜曾惠昭

執行編輯｜李迎華
封面設計｜李美瑤
美術編輯｜黃偵瑜
文字校潤｜李迎華

填寫線上回函，立即
獲得 50 元購書金。

創 辦 人｜陳銘民
發 行 所｜晨星出版有限公司
　　　　　台中市 407 工業區 30 路 1 號 1 樓
　　　　　TEL:(04)23595820　FAX:(04)23550581
　　　　　http://star.morningstar.com.tw
　　　　　行政院新聞局局版台業字第 2500 號
法律顧問｜陳思成律師
服務專線｜TEL:（02）23672044 /（04）23595819#212
傳真專線｜FAX:（02）23635741 /（04）23595493
讀者信箱｜service@morningstar.com.tw
網路書店｜http://www.morningstar.com.tw
郵政劃撥｜15060393（知己圖書股份有限公司）

初版日期｜2003 年 02 月 28 日
二版日期｜2024 年 04 月 15 日
　　ISBN｜978-626-320-809-4
　　定價｜新台幣 250 元

印　　刷｜上好印刷股份有限公司

Printed in Taiwan, all rights reserved.